## Blood

*Blood....*

I ripped open his flannel shirt, buttons pinging everywhere. His chest was awash in a sea of caked red. The hole in his chest was a dark moon in a vermilion sky.

His blood would contain alcohol, as he had been drinking. I didn't care. The blood would be pure enough. Straight from the source. The ideal way to feed. Then again, *ideal* was relative. *Ideally* I would be feasting on turkey lasagna.

I dipped my head down, placed my lips over the massive wound in his chest, and drank....

# MOON DANCE

## a Vampire for Hire novel

# BOOKS BY J.R. RAIN

Moon Dance

I Sing the Body Departed

Elvis Has *Not* Left the Building

# Moon Dance

/ / / /

J.R. Rain

Published by
Crop Circle Books
212 Third Crater, Moon

Printed in the United States of America.

First Edition

ISBN: 978-0-557-17521-5

## Dedication

This book is dedicated to mothers everywhere:
Our amazing, selfless, unsung heroes.
Love you, ma.

## Acknowledgment

I would like to thank Eve Paludan and Liisa Lee for their
generous assistance with this book.

# 1.

I was folding laundry in the dark and watching Judge Judy rip this guy a new asshole when the doorbell rang.

I flipped down a pair of Oakley wrap-around sunglasses and, still holding a pair of little Anthony's cotton briefs in one hand, opened the front door.

The light, still painfully bright, poured in from outside. I squinted behind my shades and could just made out the image of a UPS deliveryman.

And, oh, what an image it was.

As my eyes adjusted to the light, a hunky guy with tan legs and beefy arms materialized through the screen door before me. He grinned at me easily, showing off a perfect row of white teeth. Spiky yellow hair protruded from under his brown cap. The guy should have been a model, or at least my new best friend.

"Mrs. Moon?" he asked. His eyes seemed particularly searching and hungry, and I wondered if I had stepped onto the set of a porno movie. Interestingly, a sort of warning bell sounded in my head. Warning bells are tricky to discern, and I automatically assumed this one was telling me to stay away from Mr. Beefy, or risk damaging my already rocky marriage.

"You got her," I said easily, ignoring the warning bells.

"I've got a package here for you."

"You don't say."

"I'll need for you to sign the delivery log." He held up an electronic gizmo-thingy that must have been the aforementioned delivery log.

"I'm sure you do," I said, and opened the screen door and stuck a hand out. He looked at my very pale hand, paused, and then placed the electronic thing-a-majig in it. As I signed it, using a plastic-tipped pen, my signature appeared in the display box as an arthritic mess. The deliveryman watched me intently through the screen door. I don't like to be watched intently. In fact, I prefer to be ignored and forgotten.

"Do you always wear sunglasses indoors?" he asked casually, but I sensed his hidden question: *And what sort of freak are you?*

"Only during the day. I find them redundant at night." I opened the screen door again and exchanged the log doohickey for a small square package. "Thank you," I said. "Have a good day."

He nodded and left, and I watched his cute little buns for a moment longer, and then shut the solid oak door completely. Sweet darkness returned to my home. I pulled up the sunglasses and sat down in a particularly worn dining room chair. Someday I was going to get these things re-upholstered.

The package was heavily taped, but a few deft strokes of my painted red nail took care of all that. I opened the lid and peered inside.  Shining inside was an ancient golden medallion.  An intricate Celtic cross was engraved across the face of it, and embedded within the cross, formed by precisely cut rubies, were three red roses.

In the living room, Judge Judy was calmly explaining to the defendant what an idiot he was.  Although I agreed, I turned the TV off, deciding that this medallion needed my full concentration.

After all, it was the same medallion worn by my attacker six years earlier.

# 2.

There was no return address and no note. Other than the medallion, the box was empty. I left the gleaming artifact in the box and shut the lid. Seeing it again brought back some horrible memories. Memories I have been doing my best to forget.

I put the box in a cabinet beneath the china hutch, and then went back to Judge Judy and putting away the laundry. At 3:30 p.m., I lathered my skin with heaping amounts of sun block, donned a wide gardening hat and carefully stepped outside.

The pain, as always, was intense and searing. Hell, I could have been cooking over an open fire pit. Truly, I had no business being out in the sun, but I had my kids to pick up, dammit.

So I hurried from the front steps and crossed the driveway and into the open garage. My dream was to have a home with an attached garage. But, for now, I had to make the daily sprint.

Once in the garage and out of the direct glare of the summer sun, I could breathe again. I could also smell my burning flesh.

*Blech!*

Luckily, the Ford Windstar minivan was heavily tinted, and so when I backed up and put the thing into drive, I was doing okay again. Granted, not great, but okay.

I picked up my son and daughter from school, got some cheeseburgers from Burger King and headed home. Yes, I know, bad mom, but after doing chores all day, I definitely was *not* going to cook.

Once at home, the kids went straight to their room and I went straight to the bathroom where I removed my hat and sunglasses, and used a washcloth to remove the extra sunscreen. Hell, I ought to buy stock in Coppertone. Soon the kids were hard at work saving our world from Haloes and had lapsed into a rare and unsettling silence. Perhaps it was the quiet before the storm.

My only appointment for the day was right on time, and since I work from home, I showed him to my office in the back. His name was Kingsley Fulcrum and he sat across from me in a client chair, filling it to capacity. He was tall and broad shouldered and wore his tailored suit well. His thick black hair, speckled with gray, was jauntily disheveled and worn long over his collar. Kingsley was a striking man and would have been the poster boy for dashing rogues if not for the two scars on his face. Then again, maybe poster boys for rogue did have scars on their faces. Anyway, one was on his left cheek and the other was on his forehead, just above his left eye. Both were round and puffy. And both were recent.

He caught me staring at the scars. I looked away, embarrassed. "How can I help you, Mr. Fulcrum?"

"How long have you been a private investigator, Mrs. Moon?" he asked.

"Six years," I said.

"What did you do before that?"

"I was a federal agent."

He didn't say anything, and I could feel his eyes on me. God, I hate when I can feel eyes on me. The silence hung for longer than I was comfortable with and I answered his unspoken question. "I had an accident and was forced to work at home."

"May I ask what kind of accident?"

"No."

He raised his eyebrows and nodded. He might have turned a pale shade of red. "Do you have a list of references?"

"Of course."

I turned to my computer, brought up the reference file and printed him out the list. He took it and scanned the names briefly. "Mayor Hartley?" he asked.

"Yes," I said.

"He hired you?"

"He did. I believe that's the direct line to his personal assistant."

"Can I ask what sort of help you gave the mayor?"

"No."

"I understand. Of course you can't divulge that kind of information."

"How exactly can I help you, Mr. Fulcrum?" I asked again.

"I need you to find someone."

"Who?"

"The man who shot me," he said. "Five times."

# 3.

The furious sounds of my kids erupting into an argument suddenly came through my closed office door. In particular, Anthony's high-pitched shriek. Sigh. The storm broke.

I gave Kingsley an embarrassed smile. "Could you please hold on?"

"Duty calls," he said, smiling. Nice smile.

I marched through my single story home and into the small bedroom my children shared. Anthony was on top of Tammy. Tammy was holding the remote control away from her body with one hand and fending off her little brother with the other. I came in just in time to witness him sinking his teeth into her hand. She yelped and bopped him over the ear with the remote control. He had just gathered himself to make a full-scale leap onto her back, when I stepped into the room and grabbed each by their collar and separated them. I felt as if I had separated two ravenous wolverines. Anthony's fingers clawed for his sister's throat. I wondered if they realized they were both hovering a few inches off the floor. When they had both calmed down, I set them down on their feet. Their collars were ruined.

"Anthony, we do not bite in this household. Tammy, give me the remote control."

"But mom," said Anthony, in that shriekingly high-pitched voice that he used to irritate me. "I was watching 'Pokemon' and she turned the channel."

"We each get one half hour after school," Tammy said smugly. "And you were well into *my* half hour."

"But you were on the phone talking to *Richaaard*."

"Tammy, give your brother the remote control. He gets to finish his TV show. You lost your dibs by talking to *Richaaard*." They both laughed. "I have a client in my office. If I hear any more loud voices, you will both be auctioned off on eBay. I could use the extra money."

I left them and headed back to the office. Kingsley was perusing my bookshelves. He looked at me before I had a chance to say anything and raised his eyebrows.

"You have an interest in the occult," he said, fingering a hardback book. "In particular, vampirism."

"Yeah, well, we all need a hobby," I said.

"An interesting hobby, that," he said.

I sat behind my desk. It was time to change the subject. "So you want me to find the man who shot you five times. Anything else?"

He moved away from my book shelves and sat across from me again. He raised a fairly bushy eyebrow. On him, the bushy eyebrow somehow worked.

"Anything else?" he asked, grinning. "No, I think that will be quite enough."

And then it hit me. I *thought* I recognized the name and face. "You were on the news a few months back," I said suddenly.

He nodded once. "Aye, that was me. Shot five times in the head for all the world to see. Not my proudest moment."

Did he just say *aye*? I had a strange sense that I had suddenly gone back in time. How far back, I didn't know, but further enough back where men said *aye*.

"You were ambushed and shot. I can't imagine it would have been anyone's proudest moment. But you survived, and that's all that matters, right?"

"For now," he said. "Next on the list would be to find the man who shot me." He sat forward. "Everything you need is at your disposal. Nothing of mine is off limits. Speak to anyone you need to, although I ask you to be discreet."

"Discretion is sometimes not possible."

"Then I trust you to use your best judgment."

Good answer. He took out a business card and wrote something on the back. "That's my cell number. Please call me if you need anything." He wrote something under his number. "And that's the name and number of the acting homicide detective working my case. His name is Sherbet, and although I found him to be forthcoming and professional, I didn't like his conclusions."

"Which were?"

"He tends to think my attack was nothing but a random shooting."

"And you disagree?"

"Wholeheartedly."

We discussed my retainer and he wrote me a check. The check was bigger than we discussed.

"I don't mean to be rude," said Kingsley as he stood and tucked his expensive fountain pen inside his expensive jacket, "but are you ill?"

I've heard the question a thousand times.

"No, why?" I asked brightly.

"You seem pale."

"Oh, that's my Irish complexion, lad," I said, and winked.

He stared at me a moment longer, and then returned my wink and left.

# 4.

When Kingsley was gone I punched his name into my web browser.

Dozens of online newspaper articles came up, and from these I garnered that Kingsley was a rather successful defense attorney, known for doing whatever it took to get his clients off the hook, often on seemingly inane technicalities. He was apparently worth his weight in gold.

I thought of his beefy shoulders.

A lot of weight. Muscular weight.

*Down girl.*

I continued scanning the headlines until I found the one I wanted. It was on a web page for a local LA TV station. I clicked on a video link. Thank God for high speed internet. A small media window appeared on my screen, and shortly thereafter I watched a clip that had first appeared on local TV news. The clip had gone national, due to its sensationally horrific visuals.

A reporter appeared first in the screen, a young Hispanic woman looking quite grave. Over her shoulder was a picture of the Fullerton Municipal Courthouse. The next shot was a grainy image from the courthouse security camera itself. In the frame were two men and two women, all dressed impeccably, all looking important. They were crossing in front of the courthouse itself. In football terms, they formed a sort of *moving huddle,* although I rarely think of things in football terms and understand little of the stupid sport.

I immediately recognized the tall one with the wavy black hair as Kingsley Fulcrum, looking rugged and dashing.

*Down girl.*

As the group approaches the courthouse steps, a smallish man steps out from behind the trunk of a white birch. Three of the four great defenders pay the man little mind. The one who does, a blond-haired woman with glasses and big hips, looks up and frowns. She probably frowns because the little man is reaching rather menacingly inside his coat pocket. His thick mane of black hair is disheveled, and somehow even his thick mustache looks disheveled, too. The woman, still frowning, turns back to the group.

And what happens next *still* sends shivers down my spine.

From inside his tweed jacket, the little man removes a short pistol. We now know it's a .22. At the time, no one sees him remove the pistol. The short man, perhaps ten feet away from the group of four, takes careful aim, and fires.

Kingsley's head snaps back. The bullet enters over his left eye.

I lean forward, staring at my computer screen, rapt, suddenly wishing I had a bowl of popcorn, or at least a bag of peanut M&Ms. That is, until I remembered that I can no longer eat either.

Anyway, Kingsley's cohorts immediately scatter like chickens before a hawk. The shorter man even ducks and rolls dramatically as if he's recently seen duty in the Middle East and his military instincts are kicking in.

Kingsley is shot again. This time in the neck, where a small red dot appears above his collar. Blood quickly flows down his shirt. Instead of collapsing, instead of *dying* after being shot point blank in the head and neck, Kingsley actually turns and looks at the man.

As if the man had simply called his name.

As if the man had *not* shot him twice.

What transpires next would be comical if it wasn't so heinous. Kingsley proceeds to duck behind a nearby tree. The shooter, intent on killing Kingsley, bypasses going around a park bench and instead jumps over it. Smoothly. Landing squarely on his feet while squeezing off a few more rounds that appear to hit Kingsley in the neck and face. Meanwhile, the big attorney ducks and weaves behind the tree. This goes on for seemingly an eternity, but in reality just a few seconds. A sick game of tag, except Kingsley's getting tagged with real bullets.

And still the attorney does not go down.

Doesn't even collapse.

The shooter seemingly realizes he's wasting his time and dashes away from the tree, disappearing from the screen. No one has come to Kingsley's rescue. The other attorneys are long gone. Kingsley is left to fend for himself, his only protection the tree, which has been torn and shredded by the impacting stray bullets.

Witnesses would later report that the shooter left in a Ford pickup. No one tried to stop him, and I really didn't blame them.

I paused the picture on Kingsley. Blood is frozen on his cheeks and forehead, even on his open, outstretched palms. His face is a picture of confusion and horror and shock. In just twenty-three seconds, his life had been utterly turned upside down. Of course, in those very same twenty-three seconds most people would have died.

But not Kingsley. I wondered why.

# 5.

I was at the Fullerton police station, sitting across from a homicide detective named Sherbet. It was the late evening, and most of the staff had left for the day.

"You're keeping me from my kid," he said. Sherbet was wearing a long sleeved shirt folded up at the elbows, revealing heavily muscled forearms covered in dark hair. The dark hair was mixed with a smattering of gray. I thought it looked sexy as hell. His tie was loosened, and he looked irritable, to say the least.

"I apologize," I said. "This was the only time I could make it today."

"I'm glad I can work around your busy schedule, Mrs. Moon. I wouldn't want to inconvenience you in any way."

His office was simple and uncluttered. No pictures on the wall. Just a desk, a computer, a filing cabinet and some visitor's chairs. His desk had a few picture frames, but they were turned toward him. From my angle, I could only see the price tags.

I gave him my most winning smile. "I certainly appreciate your time, detective." I had on plenty of blush, so that my cheeks appeared human.

The smile worked. He blushed himself. "Yeah, well, let's make this quick. My kid's playing a basketball game tonight, and I wouldn't want to miss him running up and down the court with no clue what the hell is going on around him."

"Sounds like a natural."

"A natural dolt. Wife says I should just leave him alone. The trouble is, if I leave him alone, he tends to want to play Barbies with the neighborhood girls."

"That worries you?" I asked.

"Yeah."

"You think he could turn out gay?"

He shrugged uncomfortably, and said nothing. It was a touchy subject for him, obviously.

"How old is your son?" I asked.

"Eight."

"Perhaps he's a little Casanova. Perhaps he sees the benefits of playing with girls, rather than boys."

"Perhaps," said Sherbet. "For now, he plays basketball."

"Even though he's clueless."

"Where there's a will there's a way."

"Even if it's your will and your way?" I asked.

"For now, it's the only way." He paused, then looked a little confused. He shook his head like a man realizing he had been mumbling out loud. "How the hell did we get on the subject of my kid's sexuality?"

"I forget," I said, shrugging.

He reached over and straightened the folder in front of him. The folder hadn't been crooked, now it was less uncrooked. "Yeah, well, let's get down to business. Here's the file. I made a copy of it for you. It's against procedures to give you a copy, but you check out okay. Hell, you worked for the federal government. And why the hell you've gone private is your own damn business."

I reached for the file, but he placed a big hand on it. "This is just between you and me. I don't normally give police files to private dicks."

"Luckily I'm not your average private dick."

"A dick with no dick," he said.

"Clever, detective," I said.

"Not really."

"No, not really," I admitted. "I just really want the file."

He nodded and lifted his palm, and I promptly stuffed the file into my handbag. "Is there anything you can tell me that's perhaps not in the file?"

He shook his head, but it was just a knee-jerk reaction. In the process of shaking his head, he was actually deep in thought. "It should all be in there." He rubbed the dark stubble at his chin. The dark stubble was also mixed with some gray. "You know I always suspected the guy doing the shooting was a client of his. I dunno, call it a hunch. But this attorney's been around a while, and he's pissed off a lot of people. Trouble is: who's got the time to go through all of his past files?"

"Not a busy homicide detective," I said, playing along.

"Damn straight," he said.

"Any chance it was just a random shooting?" I asked.

"Sure. Of course. Those happen all the time."

"But you don't think so."

"No," he said.

"Why?" I asked.

The detective was used to this kind of exchange. He worked in a business where if you didn't ask questions, you didn't find answers. If my questions bothered him, he didn't show it, other than he seemed to be impatient to get this show on the road.

"Seemed premeditative. And no robbery attempt. Also seemed to be making a statement, as well."

"By shooting him in the face?"

"And by shooting him outside the courthouse. His place of work. Makes you think it was business related."

I nodded. Good point. I decided not to tell the detective he had a good point. Men tend to think all of their points were good, and they sure as hell didn't need me to boost their already inflated egos.

I'm cynical that way.

He stood from his desk and retrieved a sport jacket from a coat rack. He was a fit man with a cop's build. He also had a cop's mustache. He would have looked better without the mustache, but it wasn't was my place to suggest so. Besides, who better to wear a cop mustache than a cop?

"Now it's time to go watch my son screw up the game of basketball," he said.

"Maybe basketball's not his game."

"And playing with girls is?"

"It's not a bad alternative," I said, then added. "You think there's a chance you're reading a little too much into all of this with your son?"

"I'm a cop. I read too much into everything." He paused and locked his office door, which I found oddly amusing and ironic since his office was located in the heart of a police station. "Take you, for instance."

I didn't want to take me for instance. I changed the subject. "I'm sure you're a very good officer. How long have you been on the force?"

He ignored my question. "I wondered why you insisted on meeting me in the evening." As he spoke, he placed his hand lightly at the small of my back and steered me through the row of cluttered desks. His hand was unwavering and firm. "When I asked you on the phone the reason behind the late meeting you had mentioned something about being busy with other clients. But when I called your office later that day to tell you that I was going to be delayed, you picked up the phone immediately." He paused and opened a clear glass door. On the door was etched FPD. "Perhaps you were meeting your clients in the office. Or perhaps you were in-between clients. But when I asked if you had a few minutes you sounded unharried and pleasant. *Sure*, you said, *how can I help you?*"

"Well, I pride myself on customer service," I said.

He was behind me, and I didn't see him smile. But I sensed that he had done so. In fact, I *knew* he had smiled. Call it a side effect.

He said, "Now that I see you, I see you have a skin disorder of some type."

"Why, lieutenant, you certainly know how to make a girl feel warm and fuzzy."

"And that's the other thing. When I shook your hand, it felt anything but warm and fuzzy," he said.

"So what are you getting at?" I asked. We had reached the front offices. We were standing behind the main reception desk. The room was quiet for the time being. Outside the smoky gray doors, I could see Commonwealth Avenue, and across that, Amerige City Park, which sported a nice little league field.

He shrugged and smirked at me. "If I had two guesses, I would say that you were either a vampire, or, like I said, you had a skin condition."

"What does your heart tell you?" I asked.

He studied me closely. Outside, commuters were working their way through downtown Fullerton. Red taillights burned through the smoky glass. Something passed across his gaze. An understanding of some sort. Or perhaps wonder. Something. But then he grinned and his cop mustache rose like a referee signaling a touchdown.

"A skin disease, of course," he said. "You need to stay out of the sun."

"Bingo," I said. "You're a hell of a detective."

And with that I left. Outside, I saw that my hands were shaking. The son-of-a-bitch had me rattled. He was one hell of an intuitive cop.

I hate that.

# 6.

I was boxing at a sparring club in Fullerton called Jacky's. The club was geared towards women, but there were always a few men hanging around the club. These men often dressed better than the women. I suspected homosexuality. The club gave kick-boxing and traditional boxing lessons. I preferred the traditional boxing lessons, and always figured that if the time came in a fight that I had to kick, there was only one place my foot was going.

*Crotch City.*

I come here three times a week after picking the kids up from school and taking them to their grandmother's home in Brea. Boxing is perhaps one of the most exhausting exercises ever invented, especially when you box in three-minute drills, as I was currently doing, which simulated actual boxing rounds.

My trainer was an Irishman named Jacky. Jacky wore a green bandanna over a full head of graying hair. He was a powerfully built man of medium height, a little fat now, but not soft. He must have been sixty, but looked forty. He was an ex-professional boxer in Ireland, where he had been something of a legend, or that's what he tells me. His crooked nose had been broken countless times, which might or might not have been the result of boxing matches. Maybe he was just clumsy. Amazingly enough, the man rarely sweat, which was something I could not claim. As my personal trainer, his sole responsibility was to hold out his padded palms and to yell at me. He did both well. All with a thick Irish accent.

"C'mon, push yourself. You're dropping your fists, lass!"

Dropping one's fists was a big no-no in Jacky's world, on par with his hatred for anything un-Irish.

So I raised my fists. Again.

During these forty-five minutes workouts with Jacky, I hated that little Irish bastard with all my heart.

"You're dropping your hands!" he screamed again.

"Screw you."

"In your dreams, lass. Get them hands up!"

It went on like this for some time. Occasionally the kickboxers would glance over at us. Once I slipped on my own sweat, and Jacky thankfully paused and called for one of his towel boys who hustled over and wiped down the mat.

"You sweat like a man," said Jacky, as we waited. "I like that."

"Oh?" I said, patting myself down with my own towel. "You like the sweat of men?"

He glared at me. "My wife sweats. It's exciting."

"Probably because you don't. She has to make up for the two of you."

"I don't know why I open up to you," he said.

"You call this opening up?" I asked. "Talking about sweat and boffing your wife?"

"Consider yourself privileged," he said.

We went back to boxing. We did two more three-minute rounds. Near the end of the last round, I was having a hell of a time keeping my gloved fists up, and Jacky didn't let me hear the end of it.

When we were done, Jacky leaned his bulk against the taut ropes. He removed the padded gloves from his hands. The gloves were frayed and beaten.

"Second pair of gloves in a month," he said, looking at them with something close to astonishment.

"I'll buy you some more," I said.

"You're a freak," he said. He studied his hands. They were red and appeared to be swelling before our very eyes. "You hit harder than any man I've ever coached or faced. Your hand speed is off the charts. Good Christ, your form and accuracy is perfect."

"Except that I drop my hands."

"Not always," he said sheepishly. "I've got to tell you *something* so that you think I'm earning my keep."

I reached over and kissed his smooth forehead. "I know," I said.

"You're a freak," he said again, blushing.

"You have no idea."

"I pity any poor bastard who crosses your path."

"So do I."

He held out his hands. "Now, I need to soak these in ice."

"Sorry about that."

"You kidding? It's an honor working with you. I tell everyone about you. No one believes me. I tell them I've got a woman here that could take on their best male contenders. They never believe me."

Around us the sparring gym was a beehive of activity. Both boxing rings were now being used by kick boxers. Women and men were pounding the hell out of the half dozen punching bags, and the rhythmic rattling of the speed bags sounded from everywhere.

"You know I don't like you talking about me, Jacky."

"I know. I know. They don't believe me anyway. You could box professionally with one hand behind your back."

"I don't like attention."

"I know you don't. I'll quit bragging about you."

"Thank you, Jacky."

"The last thing I want is you pissed-off at me."

I box for self-defense. I box for exercise. Sometimes I box because it's nice to have a man care so vehemently whether or not your fists are up.

I kissed his forehead again and walked out.

# 7.

I drove north along Harbor Blvd, through downtown
Fullerton and made a left onto Berkeley Street. I parked in
the visitor parking in front of the Fullerton Municipal
Courthouse, turned off my car, and sat there.

While I sat there, I drank water from a bottle. Water is
one of the few drinks my body will accept. That and wine,
although the alcohol in wine has no effect on me.

Yeah, I know. Bummer.

My hands were still feeling heavy from the boxing
workout. I flexed my fingers. I couldn't help but notice my
forearms rippling with taut muscle. I like that. I worked
hard for that, and it was something I didn't take for granted.

I sat in the minivan and watched the entrance to the
courthouse. There was little activity at this late hour. I
wasn't sure what I was hoping to find here but I like to get a
look and feel for all aspects of a case. Makes me feel
involved and informed.

And, hell, you never know what might turn up.

Two security guards patrolled the front of the building.
So where had they been at the time of Kingsley's shooting?
Probably patrolling the *back* of the building.

Behind me was a wooded area; above that were
condominiums. A bluejay swooped low over my hood and

disappeared into the branches of a pine tree. A squirrel suddenly dashed along the pine tree's limb. The jay appeared again, and dove down after the squirrel.

*Can't we all just get along?*

When the guards disappeared around a corner, I got out of the van and made my way to the court's main entrance. My legs were still shaky from the work out; my hands heavy and useless, like twin balloons filled with sand.

The courthouses consisted of two massive edifices that faced each other. Between them was a sort of grassy knoll, full of trees and stone benches. The benches were empty. The sun was low in a darkening sky.

I like darkening skies.

Shortly, I found the infamous birch tree. The tree was smallish, barely wide enough to conceal even me, let alone a big man with broad shoulders. As a shield, it was useless, as the additional bullets in Kingsley's head attested. To have relied on it for one's sole protection of a gun-wielding madman was horrifying to contemplate. So I did contemplate it. I felt Kingsley's fear, recalled his desperate attempts to dodge the flying bullets. Comical and horrific. Ghastly and amusing. Like a kid's game of cowboys and Indians gone horribly wrong.

I circled the tree and found four fairly fresh holes in the trunk. The bullets had, of course, been dug out and added to the evidence. Now the holes were now nothing more than dark splotches within the white bark. The tree and Kingsley had one thing in common: both were forever scarred by bullets from the same gun.

The attack had been brazen. The fact that the shooter had gotten away clean was probably a fluke. The shooter himself probably expected to get caught, or gunned down himself. But instead he walked away, and disappeared in a truck that no one seemed to remember the license plate of. The shooter was still out there, his job left unfinished. Probably wondering what more he had to do to kill Kingsley.

A hell of a good question.

According to the doctor's reports cited in a supplementary draft within the police report, all bullets had missed vital parts of Kingsley's brain. In fact, the defense attorney's only side effect was a minor loss in creativity. Of course, for a defense attorney, a lack of creativity could prove disastrous.

Someone wanted Kingsley dead, and someone wanted it done outside the courthouse, a place where many criminals had walked free because of Kingsley's ability to manipulate the law. This fact was not lost on me.

Detective Sherbet had only made a cursory investigation into the possibility that the shooting was related to one of Kingsley's current or past cases. Sherbet had not dug very deeply.

It was my job to dig. Which was why I make the big bucks.

I turned and left the way I had come.

# 8.

"So how often do you, like, feed?" asked Mary Lou.

Mary Lou was my sister. Only recently had she discovered that I was, like, a creature of the night. Although I come from a big family, she was the only one I had confided in, mostly because we were the closest in age and had grown up best friends. We were sitting side-by-side at a brass-topped counter in a bar called Hero's in downtown Fullerton.

I said, "Often. Especially when I see a particular fine sweep of milky white neck. Like yours for instance."

"Ha ha," she said. Mary Lou was drinking a lemon drop martini. I was drinking house Chardonnay. Since I couldn't taste the Chardonnay, why order the good stuff? And Chardonnay rarely had a reaction on my system, and it made me feel normal, sort of, to drink something in public with my sister.

Mary Lou was wearing a blue sweater and jeans. Today was casual day at the insurance office. This was apparently something that was viewed as good. She often talked about casual day; in fact, often days before the actual casual event.

"Seriously, Sam. How often?" she asked again.

I didn't say anything. I swallowed some wine. It tasted like water. My tastebuds were dead, my tongue good for only talking and kissing, and lately not even kissing. I looked over at Mary Lou. She was six years older than me, a little heavier, but then again she ate a normal diet of food.

"Once a day," I said, shrugging. "I get hungry like you. My stomach growls and I get light headed. Typical hunger symptoms."

"But you can only drink blood."

"You mind saying that a little louder?" I said. "I don't think the guy in the booth behind us quite heard."

"Sorry," she said sheepishly.

"We're supposed to keep this quiet, remember?"

"I know."

"You haven't told anyone?" I asked her again.

"No. I swear. You know I won't tell."

"I know."

The bartender came by and looked at my nearly finished glass of wine. I nodded, shrugging. What the hell, might as well spend my well-earned money on something useless, like wine.

"Have you tried eating other food?" asked Mary Lou.

"Yes."

"What happens?" she asked.

"Stomach cramps. Extreme symptoms of food poisoning. I throw it back up within minutes. Not a pretty picture."

"But you can drink wine," she said.

"It's the only thing I've found so far that I can drink," I said. "And sometimes not even that. Needs to be relatively pure."

"So no red wine."

"No red wine," I said.

My sister, with her healthy tan, put her hand on my hand. As she did so, she flinched imperceptively from the cold of my own flesh. She squeezed my fingers. "I'm sorry this happened to you, sis."

"I am too," I said.

"Can I ask you some more questions?" she asked.

"Were you just warming me up?"

"Yes and no."

"Fine," I said. "What else you got for me?"

"Does the blood, you know, have to be human blood?"

"Any mammalian blood will do," I said.

"Where do you get the blood?"

"I buy it."

"From where?" she asked.

"I have a contract with a butchery in Norco. I buy it by the month-load. It's in my freezer in the garage."

"The one with the padlock?" she asked. I think her own blood drained from her face.

"Yes," I answered.

"What happens if you don't drink blood?"

"Probably shrivel up and die."

"Do you want to change the subject?" she asked gently. She knew my moods better than anyone, even my husband. "Please."

Mary Lou grinned. She caught the attention of the bartender and pointed to her martini. He nodded. The bartender was cute, a fact not lost on my Mary Lou.

"So what case are you currently working on?" she asked, stealing glances at the man's posterior.

"You done checking out the bartender?"

She reddened. "Yes."

So I told her about my case. She remembered seeing it on TV.

"Any leads yet?" she asked, breathless. Mary Lou tended to think that what I did for a living was more exciting than it actually was. Her drink came but she ignored it.

"No," I said. "Just hunches."

"But your hunches are better than most anyone's."

"Yes," I said. "It's a side effect."

"A good side effect."

I nodded. "Hey, if I have to give up raspberry cheesecakes, I might as well get something out of the deal."

"Like highly attuned hunches."

"That's one of them," I said.

"What else?" she asked.

"I thought we were changing the subject."

"C'mon, I've never known...someone like you."

"Don't you mean some*thing*?"

"No," she said. "That's not what I mean. You're a good mother, a good wife, and a good sister. You are much more than a *thing*. So tell me, what are the other side effects?"

"You saying all that just to butter me up?"

"Yes and no," she said, grinning. "So tell me. Now."

I laughed. "Okay, you win. I have enhanced strength and speed."

She nodded. "What else?"

"I seem to be disease and sickness free."

"What about shape-changing?"

"Shape-changing?"

"Yes."

Having my sister ask if I could *shape-change* struck me as so ridiculous that I burst out laughing. Mary Lou watched me briefly, then caught on because she always catches on. Soon we were both giggling hysterically, and we had the attention of everyone in the bar. I hate having people's attention, but I needed the laugh. Needed it bad.

31

"No," I said finally, wiping the tears from my eyes. "I can't shape-change. Then again, I've never tried."

"Then maybe you *can*," she said finally, after catching her own breath.

"Honestly, I've never thought about it. There's just been too much other crap to deal with, and this...*condition* of mine doesn't exactly come with a handbook."

"So you learn as you go," said Mary Lou.

"Yes," I said. "Sort of like *The Greatest American Hero*."

"Yeah, like him."

We drank some more. My stomach was beginning to hurt. I pushed the wine aside.

"You ever going to tell me what happened to you?" Mary Lou's words were forming slower. The martinis had something to do with that. "How you became, you know, what you are?"

I looked away. "Someday, Mary Lou."

"But not today."

"No," I said. "Not today."

Mary Lou turned in her stool and faced me. Her big, round eyes were glassy. Her nose was more slender than mine, but we resembled each other in every other way. We were sisters through and through.

"So how do you do it?" she asked.

"Do what?"

"Look so normal. Act so normal. Be so normal. Hell, life's hard enough as it is without something like this coming out of left field and knocking you upside your ass. How do you do it?"

"I do it because I have to," I said. "I don't have a choice."

"Because you love your kids."

"Sometimes it's the only reason," I said.

"What about Danny?"

I didn't tell her about Danny. Not yet. I didn't tell her that my husband seemed revolted by the sight of me, that he turned his lips away lately when we kissed, that he seemed to avoid touching me at all costs. I didn't tell her that I was sure he was cheating on me and my marriage was all but over.

"Yeah," I said, looking away. "I do it for Danny, too."

# 9.

The shower was as hot as I could stand it, which would have been too hot for most people. Some of my sensitivity had left my skin, and as a result I needed hotter and hotter showers. My husband, long ago, gave up taking showers with me. Apparently he had an aversion to the smell of his own cooking flesh.

My muscles were sore and the water helped. I was thirty-seven years old, but I looked twenty-seven, or perhaps even younger. There wasn't a wrinkle on my pallid face. My skin was taut. Usually ice cold, but taut. My muscles were hard, but that could have been because I never stopped working out. After all, there is only so much one can lose of one's self, and so I was determined to maintain some normalcy. Working out reminded me of who I was and what I was trying to be.

My body was still sore from boxing, but the soreness was almost gone. I heal fast nowadays, amazingly fast. Just your average, run-of-the-mill freak show.

I stood with my back to the spray and let my mind go blank. I stood there for God knew how long until an image of Kingsley and his bloody and confused face drifted into my thoughts. It had been such an *angry* attack. Full of pent-up rage. Kingsley had pissed off someone badly. Very

34

badly. At one point in the shooting, the shooter had actually paused and looked at Kingsley with what had been thunderstruck awe, at least that's how I interpreted the grainy image. The look seemed to say: *How many times do I have to shoot you before you die?*

I had already soaped up and washed and conditioned my hair. There was nothing left to do, and now I was only wasting water. Sighing, I turned off the shower. Rare heat rose from my skin, a pleasant change for once. My skin was raw and red, and I was in my own little piece of heaven. The kids were with their sitter, and tonight I was going out with my husband. We tried to do that more and more lately. Or, rather, *I* tried to do that more and more lately. He reluctantly agreed.

Early on, after my transformation, Danny had been a saint. Someone he loved (me) was hurting and confused, and he had come to my rescue like no other.

Together we had devised schemes to let the world know I was different. It was his idea to tell the world I had developed *xeroderma pigmentosum*, a rare, and usually fatal, skin condition. With xeroderma pigmentosum, even brief exposure to sunlight can cause irreparable damage that could lead to blindness and fatal skin cancers. People eventually accepted this about me—even my own family. Yes, I hated lying, but the way I saw it, I had little choice.

Danny helped me change careers, and helped me set up my home-based private investigation business. He also explained to the kids that mommy would often be sleeping during the day and to not bother me. Finally, he helped set me up with my feed supply with the local butchery.

Danny had been a dream. But that had been then; this was now.

So tonight we were going to dinner. I would order my steak raw and do my best to participate with him. He would avert his eyes, as usual. Not a typical relationship by any means. But a relationship, nonetheless.

I found myself looking forward to tonight. I had recently read a book about how to be a better wife, how to understand your man, how to show your love in the little ways. It's amazing how we all forget what's necessary to keep a loving relationship intact. Well, I was determined to show him my appreciation.

Of course, most marriages didn't deal with the issues I have, but we would make it through, somehow.

I was still dripping and toweling off when the phone rang. I dashed out of the connecting bathroom and into the bedroom and picked up the phone on the bedside table.

"Hello," I said.

"Hi, doll."

"Danny!"

There was a pause, and I knew instinctively that I was going to get bad news. Call it my enhanced intuition, or call it whatever you want.

"I can't make it tonight," he said.

"But Danny...."

"We're backed-up at the office. I have a court case later this week, and we're not ready. I hope you understand."

"Yes," I said. "Of course."

"I love you."

"I love you, too."

"I've got to get going. Don't wait up."

That was our little joke now. Of course, being a creature of the night, all I could do lately was wait up.

He hung up the phone.

# 10.

It was evening.

I was pacing inside the foyer of my house. The muscles along my neck were tense and stiff. Outside, through the partly open curtain, I could see the upper curve of the setting sun.

I continued to pace. Breathing was always difficult at this time of day. I was making a conscious effort to inhale and exhale, to fill my lungs as completely as I could.

In and out.

Slowly.

*Keep calm, Samantha Moon. You'll be all right.*

Nevertheless, a sense of panic threatened to overcome me. The source of the panic was the sun. Or, rather, the *presence* of the sun. Because I did not, and could not, feel fully alive until that son-of-a-bitch disappeared behind the horizon.

I checked the curtain again. The sun was still burning away in all its glory.

*Crap! Had the earth stopped in mid-orbit? Was I doomed to feel half-alive for the rest of my life?*

Panic. Pure unabated panic.

I breathed.

Deeply.

Consciously.

I leaned against the door frame and closed my eyes, willing myself to relax. I reached up and rubbed my neck muscles. I continued to breathe, continued to fight the panic.

And then, after seemingly an eternity, it happened. A sense of peace and joy began in my solar plexus and spread slowly in a wave of warmth to all my extremities. My mind buzzed with happiness, pure unabated happiness, and with it the unbridled potential of the coming night. It was a natural high. Or perhaps an *un*natural high. I opened my eyes and looked out the window. The sun was gone.

As I knew it would be.

* * *

The kids were with Mary Lou and her family at Chuck E. Cheese's. I owed Mary Lou big. Danny was working late, preparing for his big court date. So what else was new?

I had not yet realized just how much my life was unraveling. It occurred to me then, as I was driving south along the 57 Freeway, that I might have to give up detecting if Danny was going to continue working so late. In the past, he would be home with the kids. Now, he rarely got home in time to see them off to bed.

The thought of not working horrified me. Like they say, idle hands are the devil's tools. By keeping myself busy, I was able to forget some of what I had become, and to keep the nightmare of my reality at bay.

But something had to give here, and it wasn't going to be Danny. He had made it clear long ago that this was *my* problem.

# Moon Dance

My windows were down. The spring evening was warm and dry. I couldn't remember the last time we had rain. I liked the rain. Perhaps I liked the rain because I lived in Southern California. Rain here was like the elusive lover who keeps you begging for more. Perhaps if I lived up north I would not like the rain so much. I didn't know. I'd never lived anywhere else.

I took the 22 East and headed toward the city of Orange. At Main Street I exited and drove past the big mall, and turned left onto Parker Avenue and into the parking lot of the biggest building in the area.

I took the elevator to the seventh floor. In the lobby, I was greeted by a pretty brunette receptionist. *Greeted* might have been too generous. Frankly, she didn't look very much like a happy camper. She was a young girl of about twenty-five, with straight brown hair that seemed to shine like silk. My hair once shone like silk; now it hung limply. Her pink sweater knit dress was snug and form-fitting, highlighting unnaturally large breasts. Did nothing for me, but then again, I am not a man. I sensed much animosity coming from her. Waves of it. I think I knew why. She was working late, and I was part of the reason she was working late.

I gave her my most winning smile. Easy on the teeth. The nameplate on her desk read: Sara Benson.

"Hi, Sara. I'm Samantha Moon, here to see Mr. Fulcrum."

"Mr. Fulcrum is waiting for you, Mrs. Moon. I'll show you to his office."

As she did so, I said, "I understand you're going to help me tonight?"

"You understand correctly."

"I would just like to express my gratitude. I'm sure you would rather be anywhere else but here."

"You have no idea," she said, and stopped before a door. "He's in here."

# 11.

Kingsley occupied a spacious corner suite, filled with lots of dark wood shelving and legal reference books. Had the blinds not been shut he would have had a grand panoramic view of Santa Ana and Orange. Thick stacks of rubberbanded folders were piled everywhere, and in one corner was a discreet wet bar. A bottle of Jack Daniel's was sitting not-so-discreetly on the counter.

"Generally, the Jack Daniel's stays *behind* the bar during office hours," said Kingsley, moving around from behind his desk and shaking my hand, which he might have held a bit longer than protocol required. Then added, "You keep strange hours, Mrs. Moon."

I removed my hand from his grip. "And you heal surprisingly well."

The scar above his eye was almost gone. Indeed, it even appeared to have *moved* a little—to the left, perhaps—but then again Mom always told me I had an overactive imagination. He saw me looking at it and promptly turned his head.

"Touché," he said. "A drink to the freaks?"

"This freak is working. No drinking." Drinking didn't effect me, but he didn't need to know that.

"Do you mind if I have one?"

"You mean *another* one?" I asked. I could it smell it on his breath.

"You are quite the detective," he said.

"Oh yeah, *that* was a hard one."

He grinned and swept past me toward the bar. "Please, make yourself comfortable."

The closest place to make myself comfortable was a client chair that was currently occupied by a giant box. "Would you prefer I sit on a pile of folders or on top of this box?" I asked, perhaps a little snottily.

Behind me, at the bar, Kingsley had started to pour himself another drink. "Forgive me. We've been so busy lately; the place is a mess. Let me get that for you."

"Don't bother," I said, setting the heavy box on the floor.

Now back behind his desk, drink in hand, Kingsley watched me carefully. He took a sip from the highball glass. The bourbon sparkled amber in the half-light. I love half-light. I watched him watching me. Something was up. Finally, he said, "That box is filled with four fifty-pound plates," he said. "Two hundred pounds. And if you throw in the other crap in the box, that's well over two hundred pounds."

"I'm not following," I said, although i suspected I knew what he was getting at.

"It was a test," he said smugly. "And you passed. Or failed. Depending how you look at it."

I said nothing. I couldn't say anything. Instead, I found myself looking at his fading scars. Not too long ago I had stepped on a thick piece of glass; the wound had healed completely in a few hours. Unlike mine, Kingsley's face had a healthy rosy glow. And he had arrived at my home in the middle of the day and had not worn extra protection from the sun. He was not like me, and yet he had survived five bullet shots to the head.

"Well," I said, "I would have been in trouble had it been too much over two hundred pounds."

He pounced. "You only work nights, Mrs. Moon. You wear an exorbitant amount of sunscreen. Your windows, I noticed, were all completely covered. You lift two hundred pounds without a moment's hesitation. Your skin is icy to the touch. And you have the complexion of an avalanche victim."

"Okay, that last one was just mean," I said.

"Sorry, but true."

"So what are you getting at?"

He leaned back and folded his hands over his flat stomach. "You're a vampire, Mrs. Moon."

I laughed. So did he. Mine was a nervous laugh; his not so much. As I gathered my thoughts for a firm rebuttal, I found myself taking a second glance around his office. Behind his desk on the wall, was a beautiful picture of the full moon taken by a high-powered telescopic lens. There was a silver moon globe next to his monitor. Half moon bookends, which, if placed together, would form a full moon. On his desk was a picture of a woman, a very beautiful woman, with a full moon rising over her shoulder.

"You're obsessed with moons," I said.

"Which is why I picked you out of the phone book," he said, grinning. "Couldn't help myself, Mrs. Moon."

We were both silent. I watched him carefully. His mouth was open slightly. He was breathing heavily, his wet tongue pushed up against his incisors. His face looked healthy, vigorous and...feral.

"You're a werewolf," I said finally.

He grinned, wolf-like.

43

# 12.

Kingsley moved over to the window, pulled aside the blinds, and peered out into the night. With his back to me, I could appreciate the breadth and width of his shoulders.

"Could you imagine in your wildest dream," he said finally, "of ever having this conversation?"

"Never."

"And yet neither one of us has denied the other's accusations."

"Nor have we admitted to them," I added.

We were silent again, and I listened to the faint hum of traffic outside the window. I spied some of the reassuring darkness through the open slats. I was in uncharted territory here, and so I decided to roll with the situation.

"For simplicity's sake," he said, his back still to me, "let's assume we are vampires and werewolves. Where does that leave us?"

"Obviously I must kill you," I said.

"I hope you're kidding."

"I am."

"Good, because I don't die easily," he said. "And certainly not without a fight."

"I just love a good fight," I said.

He ignored me. "So," he said, turning away from the window and crossing his arms across his massive chest. "How do you want to handle this?"

"Handle what?"

He three back his head and laughed. It was a very animalistic gesture. He could have just as easily been a coyote—or a wolf—howling at the moon. "This new wrinkle in our working relationship," he said.

"As far as I'm concerned you are still my client and I'm still your detective. Nothing has changed."

"Nothing?"

"Other than the fact that you claim to be a werewolf."

"You don't believe me?"

"Mr. Fulcrum, werewolves are fairytales."

"And vampires aren't?"

I laughed. Or tried to. "I'm not a vampire. I just have a *condition*."

"A condition that requires you to stay out of the sun," he said, incredulously. "A condition that requires you to drink blood. A condition that has turned you whiter than a ghost. A condition that has given you superhuman strength."

"I never said it was a *common* condition. I'm still looking into it."

He grinned. "It's called vampirism, my dear, and it's time for you to own it."

"Own it?"

"Isn't that what the kids say these days?" he said.

"Just how old are you, Mr. Fulcrum?"

"Never mind that," he said. "The question on the table is a simple one: do you believe I'm a werewolf?"

"No," I said.

"Do you believe you are a vampire?" he asked.

I hesitated. "No."

"Fine," he said. "Is your husband cheating on you?"

"Why would you say that?" I asked.

"I assume he is," said Kingsley. "I assume he's terrified of you and he doesn't know what to do about it yet, especially with the kids in the picture."

"Shut up, Kingsley."

"And since you're not denying it, I will also go as far as to assume he's a son-of-a-bitch for abandoning you in the hour of your greatest need."

"Please, shut up."

"I also know something else, Mrs. Moon. He will take the kids from you and there isn't a single goddamn thing you can do about it."

Something came over me, something hot and furious. I flashed out of the client chair and was on Kingsley before he could even uncross his arms. My left hand went straight for his throat, slamming him hard against the wall. Too hard. The back of his head crashed through the drywall. Teeth barred, I looked up into his face—and the asshole was actually grinning at me, with half his head still in the wall. His hair and shoulders were covered in plaster dust.

*"Shut the hell up!"* I screeched.

"Sure. You got it. Whatever you say."

We stood like that for a long time, my hand clamped over his throat, his head pushed back into the wall.

"Can you set me down now?" he asked in a raspy voice.

"Down?" I said, confused, my voice still raspy in my throat.

"Yeah," he said, pointing. "Down."

I followed his finger and saw that his feet were dangling six inches above the floor. I gasped and dropped him as his head popped out of the wall.

"Sorry," I said sheepishly. "I was mad."

Kingsley rubbed his neck. "Remind me next time not to piss you off," he said, dusting off his shoulders and opening his office door. "Oh, and I'm sorry to inform you, Mrs. Moon, that you are very much a vampire."

Eyes glowing amber, he winked at me and left.

# 13.

Sara and I spent the next three hours sorting through files and since Sara was a little on the grumpy side, I did what any rational person would do under similar circumstances. I ordered Chinese. When it arrived she perked up a little. Some people needed alcohol to loosen up, apparently Sara needed fried wontons.

We ate at here desk. Or, rather, I *pretended* to eat at her desk. We ate mostly in silence.

Interestingly, according to the pictures on Sarah's desk, she seemed to know how to let loose just fine. There were pictures of her in a bikini on some tropical isle, of her hiking along a heavily forested mountain trail, of her viciously spiking a volleyball, of her dressed as a pirate in an office Halloween party, complete with massive gold hoops, eye patch and mustache. In the background was Kingsley dressed as a werewolf. I almost laughed.

"You played volleyball?" I asked.

"Yes, at Pepperdine. I tried out for the Olympics."

"What happened?"

"Almost made the team. Maybe next time."

"Maybe next time," I said. "Is Kingsley a good boss?"

She shrugged. "He's kind enough. Gives big bonuses."

"What more could you want?" I asked cheerily.

She shrugged and turned her attention to her food. I tried another approach. "Do you like your job?"

She shrugged again and I decided to let my attempt at idle conversation drop. Maybe she needed more fried wontons.

While we ate, we worked from a long list of all of Kingsley's closed files from the past six years. Seven hundred and seventy-six in all. Kingsley was a busy boy. From these files, I removed all those in which Kingsley's firm had actually *lost* the case. Now we were down to forty-two. Of these forty-two, I removed all the files in which Kingsley himself had personally litigated and lost. Now we were down to twelve. I told Sara I would need copies of all twelve files. She promptly rolled her eyes.

While we made copies, Sara decided to open up a little to me. Okay, maybe she hadn't *decided* so much as *gave in* to my constant barrage of questions. Anyway, I gleaned that she had come here to Kingsley's firm straight from college. Initially, she had loved working for her boss, but lately not so much.

"Why?" I asked, hoping for more than just a shrug. I had the Chinese restaurant's number in my pocket should I need an emergency order of fried wontons.

Turns out I didn't need the number. Rather heatedly, Sara told me in detail the story of the rapist who had been freed because Kingsley had discovered evidence of tampering at the crime scene. She finished up with: "Yes, Mr. Fulcrum's a good man. But he's a better defense attorney. And that's the problem."

I was sensing much hostility here. We were standing at the copier, working efficiently together, passing folders back and forth to each other as we copied them. Sara was very pretty and very young. Any man's dream, no doubt. She was taller than me and her breasts appeared fake, but in Southern California that's the norm and not the exception. She, herself, did not seem fake. She seemed genuine and troubled, and I suddenly knew why.

"You dated Kingsley," I said.

She looked up, startled. "Why? Did he say something to you?"

"No. Just a hunch."

She passed me another folder. I removed the brackets and flipped through it, looking for papers of unusual sizes, or POUS's, that would jam the copier. As she spoke, she crossed her arms under her large chest and leaned a hip against the copy machine. "Yeah, we dated for a while. So?"

"So what happened?" I asked.

"Ask *him*. He broke it off."

"Why?"

"You ask a lot of questions," she said.

"It's a compulsion," I said. "I should probably see a shrink about it."

Her eyes brightened a little and she nearly smiled, but then she got a handle on herself and remembered she didn't like me. "He said things were moving *too fast* for him. That he had lost his wife not too long ago and he wasn't ready for something serious."

"When did his wife die?" I asked.

"A few years ago. I don't know." She shrugged. She didn't know, and she clearly didn't care.

"Are you still angry with him?" I asked.

She shrugged and looked away and clammed up the rest of the night. Yeah, I think she was still angry.

We finished copying all twelve files, many of which were nearly a foot thick. Maybe within one I would find a suspect or a clue or *something*. At any rate, the files would give me something to do during the wee hours of the night, especially since I had recently finished Danielle Steel's latest novel, *Love Bites*, about two vampires in love. Cute, and uncannily dead on.

So Sara and I loaded up the files into a box and as I carried the entire thing out to the elevator, the young assistant watched me with open-mouthed admiration. I get that a lot.

"Jesus, you're strong," she said as we stepped into the elevator.

"It's the Pilates," I said. "You should try them."

"I will," she said. "Oh, and I'm supposed to remind you that these files are confidential."

"I'll guard them with my life."

Outside, in the crisp night air, Sara said, "I sure hope you find out who shot Knighty." She caught the indiscretion and turned beat red, her face glowing brightly under the dull parking lot lamps. "I mean, Mr. Fulcrum."

I smiled at her slip. "I do, too."

She thanked me for the Chinese food, seemed to want to tell me something else, thought better of it, then dashed off to her car. I watched her get in and back out and drive away. Just as I shoved the box into the minivan, the fine hairs at the back of my neck sprang to life. I paused and slowly turned my head. My vision is better at night. Not great, but better. I was alone in the parking lot. Check that; there was an old Mercedes parked in a parking lot across the street. A man was sitting there, and he was watching me with binoculars.

I slammed the minivan's door and moved purposely through the parking lot, crossed the sidewalk, stepped down the curb and headed across the street.

He waited a second or two, watching me steadily, then reached down and gunned his vehicle to life. Hid headlights flared to life, and before I was halfway across the street, he reversed his Mercedes and tore recklessly through the parking lot. As he exited at the far end, turning right onto Parker Avenue and disappearing down a side street, I was certain of two things:

One: he had no plates. Two: those weren't binoculars.

They were night-vision goggles.

# 14.

With the files in my backseat and thoughts of the night vision goggles on my mind, I called Mary Lou around 10:30 to thank her for watching me kids.

"I'm still watching them," she said sleepily.

"What do you mean?" I asked.

"Danny never showed up," she said.

"Did he at least call?" I asked.

"No."

I was on the 57 freeway, but instead of getting off at my exit on Yorba Linda Blvd, I continued on to Mary Lou's house two exits down. Yeah, it's nice to have family close by, especially when you have kids.

"I'm so sorry," I said when she opened the door. "I didn't mean to stick you with the kids all night."

"Not your fault. I love them, anyway. Tell me you at least made some headway on your case."

"Some headway," I admitted. I left out the part about Kingsley being a werewolf but did mention the guy in the parking lot.

"Maybe he was just some creep," said Mary Lou, frowning. "I mean you are, after all, a hot piece of ass."

"Always nice to hear from your sister," I said.

"I say don't let it worry you."

"I won't," I said. "I can take of myself."

"I know," she said. "That's what worries me."

With the kids in the backseat sleeping, I called Danny's office. He wasn't there; I left a voice mail message. Next I called his cell phone and he answered just before it went to voice mail. He sounded out of breath. Something was wrong here and warning bells sounded loud and clear in my head. I did my best to ignore them, although I couldn't ignore the fact that I had suddenly gotten sick to my stomach.

"Where are you?" I asked.

"Working late," he answered huskily.

"You doing push ups?" I said, trying to smile.

"Just ran up a flight of stairs. Bathroom on this floor isn't working."

"You didn't pick up your work phone."

"You know I never pick up after hours."

"You used to," I said.

"Well, honey, that was before I became so goddamn busy. Can I call you later?"

"Even better, why don't you *come home*."

"I'll be home soon."

He clicked off and I was left staring down at my cell phone. If it was possible, he seemed to have been breathing even harder by the end of the conversation.

* * *

It was past midnight, and I had worked my way through more than half of the sixteen files when Danny finally came home. He stopped by the study and gave me a little wave. He looked tired. His dark hair was slightly disheveled. His tie was off. The muted light revealed the deepening lines around his mouth and eyes. His eyes, once clear blue and gorgeous, were hooded and solemn. His full lips were made for kissing, but not me, not anymore. He was a handsome man, and not a very happy one.

"Sorry about not picking up the kids," he said. He didn't sound very sorry. He didn't sound like he gave a shit at all. "I should have called your sister."

"That's okay. I'll make it up to her," I said. There was lipstick on his earlobe. He probably didn't think to check his earlobe.

He said, "I'm taking a shower, then hitting the hay. Another big day tomorrow."

"I bet."

He stood there a moment longer, leaning against the door frame. He seemed to want to say something. Maybe he wanted to tell me about the lipstick.

Then he slid away, but before he was gone, I caught a hint of something in his eyes. Guilt. Pain. Confusion. It was all there. I didn't think I needed any heightened sixth sense to know that my husband of fourteen and a half years had fallen out of love with me. We all change, I suppose. Some of us more than others.

After he was done showering, I listened to the box springs creak as he eased into bed and I set down my pen and silently cried into my hands.

# 15.

I was running along Harbor Blvd at 3:00 a.m. I had finished reading through the files and needed some time to think. Luckily, I had all night to do so. Being a vampire is for me a nightly battle in dealing with loneliness.

I was dressed in full jogging gear, sweats and sweatshirt. No reflective shoes. I had been pulled over once too often by cops who had advised against a woman running so late at night. I wondered if they would give the same advice to a vampire. Anyway, I kept to the shadows, avoiding the cops and everyone else.

I kept up a healthy pace. In fact, my healthy pace was nearly a flat-out sprint. An un-godly pace that I could keep up for hours on end, and sometimes I did. Sure, my muscles hurt afterward, forcing me to soak in my hot tub. But I love the speed.

Harbor Blvd sped past me. I breathed easily. The air was suffused with mist and dew. My arms pumped rhythmically at my side, adding balance to my churning legs. Harbor was empty of all traffic and life. I made a right down Chapman, headed past the high school and junior college. Streets swept past me, I dodged smoothly around lamp poles, bus benches, and metal box thingies that had something to do with traffic lights. I think. Anyway, there seemed to be a lot of those metal box thingies.

I didn't need water and I didn't need to pause for air. It was an unusual sense of freedom. To run without exhaustion. The city was quiet and silent. The wind passed rapidly over my ears.

I was a physical anomaly. Enhanced beyond all reason. My husband once called me a super hero after seeing an example of my strength and marveling at it.

There was a half moon hanging in the sky. I thought of Kingsley and his obsession with moons. It stood to reason that a werewolf would be obsessed with moons. I ran smoothly past an open-all-night donut shop. The young Asian donut maker looked up, startled, but just missed me. The smell of donuts was inviting, albeit nauseating.

A *werewolf?*

I shook my head and chuckled at the absurdity of it. But there it was, staring me in the face. Or, rather, *he* had stared me in the face. So what was happening around here? Since when was Orange County a haven for the undead? I wondered what else was out there. Surely if there were werewolves and vampires there might be other creatures that went bump in the night, right? Maybe a ghoul or two? Goblins perhaps? Maybe my trainer Jacky was really an old, cantankerous leprechaun.

I smiled.

Thinking of Kingsley warmed my heart. This concerned me. I was a married woman. A married woman should not feel such warmth toward another man, even if the other man was a werewolf.

That is, not if she wanted to stay married. And I really, really wanted to stay married.

Perhaps I felt connected to Kingsley, bonded by our supernatural circumstances. We had much in common. Two outcasts. Two creatures ruled by the night, in one way or another.

A car was coming. I ducked down a side street and moved along a row of old homes. Heavy branches arched overhead. With my enhanced night vision, I deftly avoided irregularities in the sidewalk—cracks and upheavals— places where tree roots had pushed up against the concrete. To my eye, the night was composed of billions and billions of dancing silver particles. These silver particles illuminated the darkness into a sort of surreal molten glow, touching everything.

I turned down another street, then another. Wind howled over my ears. I entered a tougher part of town, running along a residential street called Bear. Bear opens up to a bigger street called Lemon. I didn't give a crap how tough Bear Street was.

Yet another side benefit: *unlimited courage.*

My warning bells sounded, starting first as a low buzz in my ears. The buzzing is always followed by an increase in heart rhythm, a physical pounding in my chest. I knew the feeling well enough to trust it by now, and I immediately began looking for trouble. And as I rounded another corner, there it was.

Three men stepped out of the shadows in front of me. I slowed, then finally stopped. Four more men stepped out from behind a raised truck parked on the street. Next to the house was an empty, dark school yard. As if reading their collective minds, I had a fleeting prognostication of my immediate future: an image of the seven men dragging me into the school yard. Then having their way with me. Then leaving me for dead.

## Moon Dance

A good thing the future isn't written in stone.
I smiled at them. "Hello, boys."

# 16.

Four of the seven were Latinos, with the remaining three being Caucasian, Asian and African-American. A veritable melting pot of gang violence. I studied each face. Most were damp with sweat. Eyes wide with anticipation and sexual energy. Details stood out to me like phosphorescent black and white photos, touched by ghostly silver light. One was terrified, jerking his head this way and that, like a chicken on crack. All of them around same age—perhaps thirty—save for one who was as old as fifty. A few had bed-head, as if they had been recently roused from a drunken stupor.

I could smell alcohol on their breaths and sweat on their skin. The sweat was pungent and laced with everything from fear and excitement, to hostility and sexual frustration. None of it smelled good. If *mean* had a scent, this would be it.

A smallish Latino stepped forward. A switchblade sprang open at his side, locked into place. For my benefit, he let the faint light of the moon gleam off its polished surface. He was perhaps thirty-five and wore long denim shorts and a plaid shirt. He was surprisingly handsome for a rapist.

"If you scream, I'm going to hurt you." His accent was thick.

"Gee, what a romantic thing to say," I said.

"Shut up, bitch."

I kept my eyes on him. I didn't need to look at the others. I could feel them, *sense* them, smell them. I said, "Now what would your mothers all think of you now? Ganging up on a single woman in the middle of the night. Tsk, tsk. Really, I think you should all be ashamed."

The little Latino looked at me blankly, then said simply: "Get her."

Movement from behind. I turned, punched, extending my arm straight from my body. Jacky would have been proud. My fist caught the guy in the throat. He flopped down, gagging and holding his neck. Probably hurt like hell. I didn't care.

I surveyed the others, who had all stopped in their tracks. "So what was the plan, boys? You were all going to get a fuck in? The very definition of sloppy seconds—hell, sloppy thirds and fourths and fifths. Then what? Slit my throat? Leave me for dead? Let some school janitor find me stuffed in a dumpster? You would deny my children their mother for one night of cheap thrills?"

No one said anything. They looked toward their leader, the slick Latino with the switch. Most likely not all of them spoke English.

"I'll give you once chance to run," I said. "Before I kill all of you."

They didn't run. Some continued looking at their leader. Most were looking at the man rolling on the ground, holding his throat. Switchblade was watching me with a mixture of curiosity, lust and hatred.

Then he pounced, slashing the blade up. Had he hit home, I would have been cleaved from groin to throat.

He didn't hit home.

I turned my body and the blade missed. I caught his over-extended arm at the elbow and twisted. The elbow burst at the joint. He dropped the knife. I picked him up by the throat. Screaming and gagging, he swung wildly at me with his good arm, connecting a glancing blow off the side of my head. I simply squeezed harder and his flailing stopped.

His face was turning purple; I liked that.

I raised him high and swung him around so that the others could see. They gaped unbelievingly.

"You may run now," I said.

And they did. Scattering like chickens before the hawk. They disappeared into the night, around hedges and into dark doorways. Two of them just continued running down the middle of the street. All of them were gone, save for one, the fifty year-old. He was pointing a gun at my head.

"Put my nephew down," he said.

"It's always nice to see gang raping and murdering kept in the family," I said.

I put his nephew down. Sort of. I hurled the kid with all my strength into his uncle. The gun went off, a massive explosion that rattled my senses and stung the hell out of my hyper-sensitive ears.

When the smoke cleared so to speak, the old man was looking down with bewildered horror.

Switchblade was lying sprawled on the concrete sidewalk, blood pumping from a wound in his chest. Spreading fast over the concrete. A black oil slick in the night.

*Blood.*

Something awakened within me.  Something not very nice.

The older man looked from me to Switchblade, then at the gun in his hand.  A look of horror crossed his features and tears sprang from his eyes.  Then he fled into the shadows with the others, looking back once over his shoulder before disappearing over someone's backyard fence.

I was left alone with Switchblade.  His right hand was trying to cover the wound; instead, it just flopped pathetically.

"Well," I said to him, kneeling down, "nice set of friends you have."

And as I squatted next to him, the flopping stopped and he looked at me with dead eyes.  I checked for a pulse. There was none.

Aroused by the gunshot, house lights began turning on one by one.  I looked down at the body again.

*So much blood....*

# 17.

We were alone in an alley behind some apartments.

The early morning sky was still black, save for the faint light from the half moon. I was nestled between a Dumpster and three black bags of trash filled with things foul. A small wind meandered down the alley. The plastic bags rustled. My hair lifted and fell—and so did the hair on the dead guy.

After my runs, I usually feed on cow blood. The cow blood is mixed with all sorts of impurities and foul crap. I often gag. Sort of my own private *Fear Factor* with no fifty grand reward at the end of the hour.

Before me lay Switchblade, the punk who had no doubt organized the gang bang. I had ferreted away before anyone could investigate the shooting and now he lay at my feet, dead and broken.

I looked down at his chest, where blood had stained his flannel shirt nearly black.

*Blood....*

I ripped open his flannel shirt, buttons pinging everywhere. His chest was awash in a sea of caked red. The hole in his chest was a dark moon in a vermilion sky.

His blood would contain alcohol, as he had been drinking. I didn't care. The blood would be pure enough. Straight from the source. The ideal way to feed. Then again, *ideal* was relative.  *Ideally* I would be feasting on turkey lasagna.

I dipped my head down, placed my lips over the massive wound in his chest, and drank....

* * *

I returned the body to the same house, left it where it had fallen.  I drifted back into the darkness of the school grounds, where I knew in my heart they were going to drag me off to be raped.

It was still early morning, still dark.  No one was out on the streets.  Curious neighbors had gone back to sleep; there were no police investigating the sound of a gunshot.  Apparently gunshots here were a common enough occurrence to not arouse *that* much suspicion.

The attackers themselves were long gone.  They were scared shitless, no doubt.  One of their own had been shot by one of their own.  Each would awaken this morning from a very bad hang over, and pray to God this had all been a very bad dream.

Instead of their prayers being answered, they were going to awaken to find the body.  What happened next, I didn't really know or care.  I doubted a group of men would even attempt to identify me, lest they reveal the nature of their true intentions the night before.

At any rate, using a half empty can of beer from the nearby dumpster, I had cleaned the wound of my lip imprints.  Let the medical examiner try to figure out why someone had sloshed beer all over the gunshot wound.

As I stood there in the darkness, with a curious phantasmagoric mist nipping at my ankles, I remembered the taste of his blood again.

*God, he had tasted so good. So damn good—and pure. The difference between good chocolate and bad chocolate. The difference between good wine and bad wine. Good blood and bad blood.*

All the difference in the world.

I left the school grounds and the neighborhood as a slow wave of purple blossomed along the eastern horizon. I hated the slow wave of purple that blossomed along the eastern horizon. The sun was coming, and I needed to get home ASAP.

Already I could feel my strength ebbing.

Since my belly was full of Switchblade's blood, I did not want to cramp up and so I kept my jog slow and steady. On the way home, as the guilt set in over what I had just done, I held fast to one thought in particular as if it were a buoy in a storm:

*I did not kill him; he was already dead....*

*I did not kill him; he was already dead....*

# 18.

The kids were playing in their room and Danny was working late. Tonight was Open House at the elementary school, and he had promised to make it home on time.

The words "we'll see" had crossed my mind.

I had spent the past two hours helping Anthony with his math homework. Math didn't come easily to him and he fought me the entire time. Vampire or not, I was drained.

All in all, I just couldn't believe the amount of work his third grade teacher assigned each week, and it was all I could do to keep up. Didn't schools realize mothers want to spend quality time with their children in the evenings?

So now I was in my office, still grumbling. It was early evening and raining hard. Occasionally the rain, slammed by a gust of wind, splattered against my office window. The first rain in months. The weatherman had been beside himself.

I liked the rain. It touched everything and everyone. Nothing was spared. It made even a freak like me feel connected to the world.

So with the rain pattering against the window and the children playing somewhat contentedly in their room, I eventually worked my way through all of Kingsley's files.

Only one looked promising, and it set the alarms off in my head. I've learned to listen to these alarms.

The case was no different than many of Kingsley's other cases. His client, one Hewlett Jackson, was accused or murdering his lover's husband. But thanks to Kingsley's adroit handling of the case, Jackson was freed on a technicality. Turns out the search warrant had expired and thus all evidence gathered had been deemed inadmissible in court. And when the verdict was read, the victim's brother had to be physically restrained. According to the file, the victim's brother had not lunged at the alleged killer; no, he had lunged at *Kingsley*.

There was something to that.

And that's all I had. A distraught man who felt his murdered brother had not been given proper justice. Not much, but it was a start.

I sat back in my chair and stared at the file. The rain was coming down harder, rattling the window. I listened to it, allowed it to fill some of the emptiness in my heart, and found some peace. I checked my watch. Open House was in an hour and still no sign of Danny.

I pushed him out of my thoughts and logged onto the internet; in particular, one of my many investigation data bases. There had been no mention of the brother's name in the file, but with a few deft keystrokes I had all the information I needed.

The murder had made the local paper. The article mentioned the surviving family members. Parents were dead, but there had been two surviving siblings. Rick Horton and Janet Maurice. Just as I wrote the two names down, the house phone rang. My heart sank.

I picked it up.

"Hi, dollface."

"Tell me you're on your way home," I said.

There was a pause. He sucked in some air. "Tell the kids I'm sorry."

"No," I said. "You tell them."

"Don't."

I did. I called the kids over and put them on the phone one at a time. When they were gone, I came back on the line.

"You shouldn't drag the children into this, Samantha," he said.

"Drag them into what, pray tell?"

He sighed. When he was done sighing, I heard a voice whisper to him from somewhere. A *female* voice.

"Who's that whispering to you?" I asked.

"Don't wait up."

"Who's that—"

But he disconnected the line.

# 19.

We were late for Open House.

I had a hell of a time getting the kids ready, and had long ago abandoned any notion of making dinner. We popped into a Burger King drive-thru along the way.

"Tell me what you guys want," I said, speaking over my shoulder. We were third in line at the drive-thru. The kids were wearing some of their best clothes, and I was already worried about stains.

I looked in the rearview mirror. The kids were separated by an invisible line that ran between their two back seats. Crossing the line was grounds for punishment. At the moment, Tammy was hovering on the brink of that line, making faces at Anthony, taunting him, sticking her tongue out, driving him into a seething rage. I almost laughed at the scene, but had to do something.

"Tammy, your tongue just crossed the line. No TV or Game Boy tonight."

Anthony said, "Yes!" Then pointed at his sister. "Ha!"

Tammy squealed. "But, mom, that's not fair! It was just my tongue!"

"Tongues count. Plus, you know better than to tease your little brother." We moved up in line. "What do you two want to eat?"

Tammy said she didn't want anything. Anthony gave me his usual order: hamburger, plain. I ordered Tammy some chicken fingers.

"I don't want chicken fingers."

"You like chicken fingers."

"But I'm not hungry."

"Then you don't have to eat them, but if you waste them, the money's coming out of your allowance. Anthony, don't tease your sister."

Anthony was doing a little victory dance in the back seat, which rocked the entire minivan. His sister had been successfully punished and he had escaped unscathed. It was a triumphant moment for younger brothers everywhere.

And just when he thought I wasn't looking, just when he thought the coast was clear, he gave his sister the middle finger. Tammy squealed. I burst out laughing. And by the time we left the drive-thru, both of them had lost two days of TV privileges.

And as I pulled out of the Burger King parking lot, Anthony wailed, "There's mustard on my hamburger!"

"Christ," I muttered, and made a U-turn and headed back through the drive-thru.

# 20.

After Open House, the three of us were sitting together on the couch watching reruns of *Sponge Bob*. Sadly enough, I had seen this episode before. Danny still wasn't home, nor did I really expect him to be any time soon.

Open House had gone well enough. Anthony was passing all his classes, but just barely. His teacher felt he spent too much time trying to be the class clown. Tammy, a few years older, was apparently boy crazy. Although her grades were just about excellent, her teacher complained she was a distraction to the other students; mostly to the male variety.

Apparently, my kids liked attention, and I wondered if I was giving them enough of it at home.

"What's that smell?" I asked.

"Whoever smelt it dealt it," said Anthony, giggling.

"Probably you," said Tammy to her brother. "You're always cutting them."

"So do you!"

"Do not! I'm a girl. Girl's don't cut anything."

"Yeah, right!" shouted Anthony.

"I don't smell anything, Mommy," said Tammy, ignoring her brother.

I proceeded to sniff armpits and feet. As I smelled, they both giggled, and Anthony tried to smell my own feet.

"It's you, mommy," he shouted, giggling. "Your feet stink!"

"Do not," I said. "Girls' feet don't stink."

"You're not a girl."

"Oh, really?"

"Then what is she, lame brain?" asked Tammy.

"She's a *lady*," said Anthony.

"Thank you, Anthony," I said, hugging his warm body. "Lady is good."

"And ladies have stinky feet," he added.

"Okay, now you just blew it," I said, and tickled the hell out of him. He cowered in the corner of the couch, kicking pillows at me, and then Tammy jumped on my back to defend her little brother and soon we were all on the floor, poking fingers at any and all exposed flesh, a big tickling free-for-all.

Later, as we lay gasping on the floor as Sponge Bob and his infamous square pants completed another fun-filled romp at the bottom of the ocean, Anthony asked, "Mommy, why are you always...cold?"

"Mommy is sick," I said. And, in a way, I was *very* sick.

"Are you going to die soon?" he asked.

"No," I said. "Mommy won't die for a very long time."

"Good!" he said.

"But can we catch what you have?" asked Tammy, always the careful one.

"No," I said. "You can't."

I suddenly wrinkled my nose. The smell was back. From my angle on the floor, I could just see under the couch. And there, in all its glory, was one of Anthony's rolled up socks. A very smelly rolled up sock. I used a pencil and pulled it out, where it hung from the tip like radioactive waste.

"Look familiar, Anthony?" I asked.

He mumbled an apology and I told him to throw it in the wash, and as he got up to do so, Tammy and made farting noises with each step he took.

Bad move.

He turned and threw the sock back at us and we spent the next few minutes playing hot potato with it, laughing until our stomachs hurt.

# 21.

After my attack six years ago, about the same time I first went online, I made a cyber friend.

I was exploring through the new and interesting world of chatrooms. I landed in a room called *Creatures of the Night*. The room was comical to a degree, for there seemed to be a running script of a vampire appearing in a castle and sucking the life out of its inhabitants. There were many rapid postings, and it was difficult to keep up. Still, one thing was obvious: everyone here loved vampires with all their heart and soul. And many wanted to *be* vampires.

A private message box had next appeared on my screen. Someone named Fang950 was trying to contact me. He said *Hi* and I responded back. Over the course of the next few hours, which flew rapidly by, I found myself opening up to the this Fang950. It was exhilarating. I told him everything. Everything. All my deepest secrets. I didn't care if he believed me or not. I didn't know him from squat. But he listened, and he asked questions and he did not judge me. He was the perfect outlet to my angst. And no one knew about him but me. No one. He was all mine.

It was late, and it was still raining. I had gone to the open house alone. Danny had yet to come home. I had already fed for the night and was sitting in my office in a bit of a stupor. I always felt sluggish after feeding, not to mention bloated and sick to my stomach.

A private message window popped up on my computer screen, followed by the sound of splashing water. It was Fang.

*You there, Moon Dance?* he wrote, referring to my screen name, the only name he knew me by.

*Yes, Fang, what's up?*

*Nothing new. How about you?*

There was never anything new with Fang. He told me little about himself. I knew only that he lived in Missouri and that he was twenty-eight.

So I spent the next few minutes catching him up on my new case. I left out names of course, but Fang was computer savvy. If he was interested enough he would find out about the story himself.

*What does your gut tell you about the file?* he asked.

*My gut tells me I'm onto something,* I answered.

*Too bad your gut can't be more specific.*

*Yes, too bad,* I wrote. *But it's helped me solve cases before, though. I've developed quite a reputation here. But I feel like I'm cheating.*

*Cheating?*

I thought about that a little, then wrote: *Well, other P.I.'s don't have the benefit of a heightened sixth sense, or whatever you want to call it.*

*But other P.I.'s work in the day,* he wrote. *You are handicapped by working nights.*

*It's not much of a handicap. I can get around it.*

*Nonetheless. Remember, you help people. That's the important thing. Whether or not you're cheating doesn't matter. It's the end result, right? Didn't you once say you turn down more cases than you accept?*

I wrote, *Yes.*
*Which cases do you turn down?* he asked.
*Cheating spouses mostly.*
*Which cases do you accept?*
*The bigger cases. Murder cases. Missing person cases.*
*How do your clients find you?*
*Police referrals mostly,* I wrote. *If the police can't solve the crime, they will sometimes send the clients my way. I have developed a reputation for finding answers.*

*You do good work. You are like a super hero. You help those who have nowhere else to turn for answers. You give them the answers.*

There it was again. Super hero.

The rain continued. I heard Danny come in, but he didn't bother to stop by my office in the back of the house. Instead, I heard him head straight into the shower. To shower *her* off him, no doubt.

*But sometimes the answers should remain hidden,* I wrote a few minutes later, distracted by Danny's appearance.

*Sometimes not,* wrote Fang. *Either way, your clients have closure.*

I nodded to myself, then wrote, *Closure is a gift.*

He wrote, *Yes. You give them that gift. So you think this distraught brother took a few shots at your client?*

*I'm thinking it's likely.* I paused in my typing, then added, *Do you believe that I am a vampire, Fang?*

*You have asked me this a hundred times,* he answered.

*And I have conveniently forgotten your answers a hundred times.*

*Yes,* he wrote. *I believe you are a vampire.*
*Why do you believe I am a vampire?*
*Because you told me you are.*

# Moon Dance

*And you believe that?*
*Yes.*

I took in some air, then typed: *I sucked the blood from a dead man last night.*

There was a long pause before he wrote: *Did you kill him, Moon Dance?*

*No, I didn't. He was already dead, part of a gang that attacked me. He was accidentally shot by someone in his gang. The shot had been intended for me.*

*OMG, are you okay?!*

I loved Fang, whoever the hell he was. I wrote, *Yes, thank you. It was nothing. The bangers didn't know with whom they were dealing.*

*Of course they didn't, how could they? So what happened to the dead guy?*

*I sucked his blood until I couldn't swallow another drop.*

There was a long pause. Rain ticked on the window.

*How did that make you feel?* he asked.

*At the time? Refreshed. Whole. Complete. Rejuvenated.*

*He tasted that good, huh?*

*Even better,* I wrote.

*How do you feel now?* he asked.

*Horrified.*

*Does it worry you that he tasted so good?*

*Not really,* I wrote. *But I do realize now how much I'm missing. Cow blood is disgusting.*

*I bet. Can you still control yourself, Moon Dance?*

*Yes. I've never lost control of myself. As long as I'm satiated each night on the blood stored in my refrigerator.*

*What would happen if you ran out of blood?*

*I don't want to think about it,* I wrote. *It's never happened, nor do I plan on it happening.*

78

*Sounds like a plan,* he wrote.

I laughed a little and sat back in my chair and drank some water. I typed, *I met a werewolf.*

*No shit?*

*No shit,* I wrote.

*What's a werewolf like?*

*I don't really know just yet. Mysterious. Obsessed with the moon.*

*Stands to reason.*

*He's a practicing attorney,* I wrote. *And a very good one.*

*Well, we all need a day gig.*

*Or a night gig,* I added.

*Haha. Well, Moon Dance, it's late. Let me know how it goes with the werewolf. When will be the next full moon?*

*A few days. I already checked.*

*Have there been any unsolved murders resembling animals attacks?* he asked.

*Not to my knowledge.*

*Might want to stay alert for that,* he said.

*True,* I wrote.

*Goodnight, Moon Dance.*

*Goodnight, Fang.*

# 22.

I was driving south on the 57 Freeway when my cell phone rang. It was Kingsley.

"Have you heard the news?" he asked excitedly.

"That you're a werewolf?" I suggested.

"Tsk, tsk, tsk, dear girl. Not over the phones lines. You never know who might be listening."

"Big Brother? Aliens? Homeland Security?"

"Hewlett Jackson's dead."

I blinked. "Your client."

"Now my ex-client."

"Murder?" I asked.

"Yes. Shot."

"Let me guess," I said. "Five times in the head."

"Close. Nine."

"Appears our killer wasn't going to take any chances this time."

"Find them," said Kingsley.

"That's my job," I said.

"You have any leads?"

"One."

"Just one?"

"That's all I need," I said.

"I see," he said. "Well, the police say you're the best. So I trust you."

There was some static, followed by a long pause. Too long.

"You there?" I asked.

"I'm here," he said, then added, "Tomorrow's a full moon, you know."

"I know," I said. "So, can I watch?"

"Watch?" he asked.

"You know, the transformation."

"No," he said. "And you're a sick girl."

"Not sick," I said. "Just were-curious."

He snorted and I could almost see him shaking his great, shaggy head. He said, "So I heard they found a corpse in Fullerton," he said, pausing. "Drained of blood."

"Tsk, tsk, tsk," I said. "Not over the phone. But if it puts you at ease, no, I didn't kill him."

"Good."

More static. More pausing. With some people, gaps in the conversation can feel uncomfortable. With Kingsley, gaps felt natural. Then again, we were immortal. Technically, we could wait forever.

Kingsley un-gapped the conversation. "So where you headed at this late hour?"

"It's early for me, and I'm following up on my one lead."

"Tell me about your lead."

So I did.

When I was finished, Kingsley said, "Yeah, I remember him. Rick Horton. His brother was dead and the only suspect was walking free because of a police screw up."

"Why, Kingsley, if I didn't know you better I would almost say you sound sympathetic."

"I wouldn't go *that* far."

"Tell me about the incident in the court," I said.

"He lunged at me, but it was sort of a half-ass effort. Mostly he called me a stream of obscenities."

"You must be used to them."

"Like they say, sticks and stones," he said. "He didn't seem the type for violence, though."

"Some never do."

"True," he said. "You know where he lives?"

"I've got his address. I still happen to have friends in high places."

"Good, let me know how it goes."

"Have fun tomorrow night," I said. *"Arr Arr Arrrooooo!"*

"Not funny," he said, but laughed anyway.

I disconnected the line, giggling.

# 23.

I took the 22 East, then headed south on the 55 and exited on Seventeenth Street. Rick Horton lived in an upscale neighborhood in the city of Tustin, about ten miles south of Fullerton. I continued following the Yahoo driving directions until I pulled up in front of a two-story Gothic revival. A house fit for a vampire.

From its triangular arches, to its cast-iron roof crestings, from its diamond-patterned slate shingles, to its multiple stacked chimneys, the Horton house was as creepy and menacing and haunted-looking as any house in Orange County. It was set well back from the road on a corner lot, surrounded by a massive ivy-covered brick and mortar fence. The fence was topped with the kind of iron spikes that would have made Vlad the Impaler proud. The entire house was composed of a sort of squared building stone.

I used the call box by the front gate. A man answered. I gave him my name and told him I was a private investigator and that I would like to speak to Rick Horton. There was a moment of silence, then the gate clicked open. I pushed it open all the way and followed a red brick path through a neat St. Augustine lawn. All in all, this brooding and romantic Victorian-era home seemed a little out of place in Tustin, California.

Just as I stepped up onto the entry porch, the door swung open. A small man with wire-rim glasses leaned through the open door. "Please come in," he said. "I'm Rick Horton."

I did and found myself in the main hall. To my right was a curving stairway. The ceiling was vaulted and there were many lit candles. The house was probably dark as hell during the day, perfect for a slumbering vampire.

I followed the little man through an arched doorway and into a drawing room. I've only been in a few formal drawing rooms, and, unlike the name suggests, there wasn't a single drawing in the place. Instead, it was covered in landscape oils. I was asked to sit on a dusty Chippendale camelback sofa, which I did. The sofa faced a three sided bay window with diamond-pane glass. The window overlooked the front lawn and a marble fountain. The fountain was of a mermaid spouting water. She easily had double-D breasts, which were probably a distinct disadvantage for real mermaids. Just outside the window three classic fluted Doric columns supporting a wide veranda.

He sat opposite me in a leather chair-and-a-half, which was perfect for cuddling. I wasn't in the cuddling mood. Rick Horton wore single gold studs in each ear. He seemed about twenty years too old to be wearing single gold studs. Call me old-fashioned. He was dressed in green-plaid pajamas, with matching top and bottom. He had the air of a recluse. Maybe he was a famous author or something.

"Do you have a license I can see?" he asked. As he spoke, he looked a bit confused and out of sorts, blinking rapidly as if I were shining a high-powered light into his eyes.

I held out my license and he studied it briefly. I hated the picture. I looked deathly ill: face white, hair back, cheeks sallow. I looked like a vampire. The make-up I had been wearing that day seemed to have evaporated with the camera's flash. The picture was also a little blurry, the lines of my face amorphous.

He sat back. "So what can I do for you, Ms. Moon?"

It was actually *Mrs.*, but you choose your battles. "I'm looking into a shooting."

"Oh? Who was shot?"

"My client; shot five times in the face." Horton didn't budge. Not even a facial twitch. "And I think you shot him, Mr. Horton."

That was a conversation killer. Somewhere in the house a grandfathers clock ticked away, echoing along the empty hallways, filling the heavy silence.

"You come into my house and accuse me of murder?" he said.

"Attempted murder," I said. "My client did not die, which is how he was able to hire me in the first place."

"Who's your client?"

His attempt at moral outrage was laughable. His heart just didn't seem into it.

"Kingsley Fulcrum," I said.

"Yes, of course, the defense attorney. It was on the news. Watched him hide behind a tree. It was very amusing. I wished he had died. But I didn't shoot him."

I analyzed his every word and mannerism on both a conscious and sub-conscious level. I waited for that psychic-something to kick in, that extra-sensory perception that gives me my edge over mere mortals, that clarity of truth that tells me on a intuitive level that *he's our man*. Frustratingly, I got nothing; just the fuzziness of uncertainty. His words had the ring of truth. And yet he still felt dirty to me. There was something wrong here.

85

"Did you hire someone to shoot Kingsley?" I asked.

"Maybe I should have an attorney present."

"I'm not a cop."

"Maybe you're wired."

"I'm not wired." Weird, but not wired.

He shrugged and sat back. "I can't express to you how happy I was to see that son-of-a-bitch get what he deserved. Trust me, if I had shot him I would be proud to say I had. But, alas, I cannot claim credit for what I didn't do."

"Did you hire someone to kill him, Mr. Horton?"

"If I had, would I tell you?"

"Most likely not, but never hurts to ask. Sometimes a reaction to a question speaks volumes." More than he realized.

"Fine. To answer your question: I did not hire someone to kill Kingsley Fulcrum."

"Where were you on the day he was shot?"

"What day was it?"

I told him.

"I was here, as usual. My father left me a sizable inheritance. I don't work. Mostly I read and watch TV. I'm not what you would call a go-getter."

"You have no alibi?"

"None."

"Do you own a .22 pistol?"

He jerked his head up. *Bingo.* "I think this interview is over, Ms. Moon. I did not shoot Mr. Fulcrum. If the police wish to question me further, then they can do so in the presence of my attorney. Good night."

I stood to leave, then paused. "Hewlett Jackson was found dead today, shot nine times in the head."

Horton inhaled and the faintest glimmer of a smile touched his lips. The look on his face was one of profound relief. "Like I said, the police can interview me with my attorney present."

I found my way out of the creepy old house. I love creepy old houses. Must be the vampire in me.

# 24.

*You there, Fang?*
*I'm here, Moon Dance.*
*I visited a suspect tonight,* I wrote. When I instant message, I tend to get right to the point.
*The one you thought might be the shooter?*
*Yeah, that one, but now I'm not so sure he was the shooter.*
Fang paused, then wrote: *Doesn't feel right?*
*I'm not sure.*
*You're getting mixed signals.*
*Yes,* I wrote. Fang was damn intuitive himself, and often very accurate in his assessments of my situations. I loved that about him. *But he feels dirty, though.*
*Well, maybe he's connected somehow.*
*Maybe. When I mentioned the gun, I got the reaction I was looking for.*
*There you go. Maybe his gun was used, but he wasn't the killer.*
*Maybe.*
There was a much longer pause. Typically, Fang and I chatted through the internet as fast as two people would talk. Perhaps even faster.
*I have a woman here,* he wrote. *She wants my attention.*

# Moon Dance

I grinned, then wrote: *Have fun.*
*I plan to. Talk to you soon.*

* * *

It was time for my feeding.

I checked on my children; both were sound asleep. I even looked in on Danny. He once slept only in boxers. Now he sleeps in full sweats and a tee-shirt. His explanation was simple: He didn't like brushing up against my cold flesh.

*Screw my cold flesh. I never asked for this.*

I walked quietly through the dark house. I didn't bother with the lights because a) I didn't need them and b) I didn't want to disturb the others. Danny recently commented that the thought of me wandering through the house at night creeped him out. Yeah, he said *creeped.* My own husband.

*Screw him, too.*

In the kitchen, I paused before the pantry. After a moment's hesitation, I opened the cupboard and reached for what I knew would be there: A box of Hostess Ding Dongs. I opened the box flap. Inside, two rows of silver disks flashed back at me. There was something very beautiful about the simplicity of the paper-thin tinfoil wrappings.

As I removed three of them, saliva filled my mouth. My heart began to race.

I sat at the kitchen table and unwrapped the first Ding Dong, wadding the foil wrapping tightly into a little silver ball. Before me, the chocolate puck gleamed dully in the moonlight. My stomach churned, seemed to turn in on itself, roiling like an ocean wave.

The first bite was small and exploratory. Christ, the chocolate tasted so damn good I could have had an orgasm.

Maybe I did. Rich and complex and probably fake, the cocoa flavor lingered long after the first bite has been swallowed.

There was no turning back now.

I quickly ate the first Ding Dong and tore into the second. When I finished it, the third. Finally, I sat back in the wooden chair and felt like a royal glutton. Granted, most of my tastebuds were gone, but chocolate somehow made it through loud and clear.

Outside, through an opening in the curtained window over the sink, the sky was awash with moonlight. Tomorrow was a full moon. Tonight it was almost there, but not quite. I wondered if the almost-but-not-quite full moon had any affect on Kingsley. Maybe a few extra whiskers here and there. Teeth and nails a bit longer than usual.

I giggled about that and considered calling and teasing him, but it was two in the morning. Life is lonely at two in the morning.

My stomach gurgled.

*Here it comes*, I thought.

I wondered again how long Kingsley had been a werewolf. I also realized he never really admitted to being one. Perhaps he was some variant of a werewolf. Perhaps a were-something else. Maybe a were-kitty.

I shifted in the chair to ease the pain growing in my stomach. Some serious cramping was setting in.

How old was he? Where was he from?

I suddenly lurched forward, gasping. I heaved myself out of the chair and over to the kitchen sink. I turned on the faucet just as the Ding Dongs came up with a vengeance, gushing north along my esophagus with alarming ferocity.

When done, I wiped my mouth and sat on the kitchen floor. I checked my watch. I had kept the Ding Dongs down for all of ninety-three seconds.

I wanted to cry.

# 25.

I don't sleep in a coffin.

I sleep in my bed, under the covers, with the blinds drawn. I go to bed the moment the kids head off to school, and wake up a couple of hours before they get out. Ideally, I could sleep through the entire cycle of the day, but I'm a mom with kids and *ideally* is out the window.

My sleep is deep and usually dreamless. It's also rejuvenating in ways that I can't fully comprehend. Prior to closing my eyes, usually minutes after my children have left for the day, I am nearly catatonic with fatigue. So much so that I sometimes wonder if I am dying—or perhaps nearly dead—and the deep sleep itself revives me, rejuvenates me, rebuilds me in supernatural ways that I will never understand.

And the moment my head hits the pillow I'm out cold. That is, until my alarm goes off at its loudest setting. I awaken grudgingly and exhausted, fully aware that I should still be sleeping, and that I should never, *ever* be seeing the light of day. Nevertheless, I do get up. I do face the light of day, and I keep trying to be the best mom I can.

My sleep is usually dreamless. But not always. Sometimes I dream that I am a great bird. I fly slowly, deliberately, my powerful wings outstretched, flapping slowly. I never seem to be in a hurry.

Sometimes I dream of my kids, that I infect them with my sickness and they become like me: Hungry for blood, shunned by society, living a secret life of fear and confusion and pain. I usually wake up crying.

Today, I did not wake up crying. Today, I woke up with a smile on my face. Yes, I was still exhausted and could have used a few more hours of sleep, but nonetheless I woke up with a happy heart.

Today, I dreamed of a man. A great hulking creature of a man with the broadest shoulders I'd ever seem and a mane of hair as thick as any wild animal. A man whose eyes glowed amber under the moonlight and whose grin was more wolf than human. In the dream, Kingsley had been stalking me in the deep dark woods. Sometimes he was half-man, and sometimes he was all wolf. The biggest wolf I'd ever seen.

In the dream, I was hiding from him, but it was a game, and I had no fear of the man-wolf. I was hiding behind the trunk of a massive pine tree as he searched the forest for me.

We seemed to do this forever, playing, and I had a sense that we *could* do this forever, if we so desired. That nothing could stop us. Ever. Finally, I stepped out from behind the tree and just stood there on the wooded path. Kingsley, the man, came to me, hunger in his amber eyes. I had forgotten about such hunger. Pushed it aside. I had assumed such a look would be forever lost to me, replaced only by Danny's disgust and horror.

But not with Kingsley. He *hungered* for me.

More important: He *accepted* me.

Then he was upon me, pouncing, taking me up in his great arms and lowering his face to mine. And as he did so, something flashed out of the corner of my eye. The golden amulet, the same one worn by my attacker years ago. I tried to ask Kingsley about the amulet but he lowered his face to mine and took me completely and wholly to a place I had never thought I would go again.

And that's when I awoke, smiling.

*Wow.*

A minute later when I had regained my senses, I got out of bed and, adverting my eyes from the light sneaking in through the blinds, made my way into the living room. There, under the china hutch, I found the box and opened it. Inside was the medallion with the three ruby roses.

I reached in and turned it over. There was blood on it. A tiny speckle that I had missed.

Why had Kingsley refused to discuss the medallion in my dream? Then again, how could he have even known about the medallion?

Then again, I reminded myself, it was just a dream.

*Better yet, why are you dreaming of another man? You are a married woman. Dreams like that could lead to trouble.*

A lot of trouble.

I returned the medallion to the box, closed the lid and smiled again.

It had been, after all, a hell of a dream.

# 26.

Before I became a full-time creature of the night, I was a federal agent for the Department of Housing and Urban Development, or HUD. Although its acronym was not as sexy-sounding as the FBI, my ex-partner and I busted our fair share of bad guys; in particular, real estate scams artist and loan swindlers and those who preyed on the poor.

Anyway, Chad Helling and I had been partners for just over two years when I had been forced to quit and find a night job. He understood. Or, rather, he understood the *given* reason.

He and I were still close, and through him I used the federal government's resources for all they were worth. In exchange, I did some pro bono investigating work for him.

Chad answered his cell on the third ring. "Hey, sunshine."

"Sunshine?" I asked.

"Sorry. Poor choice of words. What's up?"

"I need some help," I said.

"What else is new?"

I ignored that. "The name's Rick Horton out of Tustin. I need to know if he has a twenty-two caliber pistol registered to his name."

"Anything else?"

"No, that's it."

"You got it, Sunshine."

"Asshole," I said, but he had already hung up.

It was the late evening. I tried Kingsley at his office number, but was not surprised to discover that Kingsley had called in sick since this was the night of the full moon. I tried his home number. It was answered immediately.

"Tonight's the big night," I said. "Arooo!"

"Who's this?" asked a stuffy voice.

Whoops!

"I'm, uh, Samantha Moon. May I speak to Kingsley?"

A pause on the other end. I thought I heard a noise from somewhere in the background. Perhaps my imagination was playing tricks on me, but, son-of-a-bitch, I thought I had heard the howl of a dog.

Or a wolf.

"Master Kingsley is...indisposed at this time. I'll tell him you rang."

*Master Kingsley?*

"Please do," I said, trying to match the upper-crust voice. I think I warbled perhaps a little too long on *do*. The line was disconnected, and not by me.

Almost immediately my cell vibrated in my hand. I looked at the face-plate. It was my ex-partner.

"Yup, a twenty-two caliber pistol is registered to one Rick Horton," said Special Agent Chad Helling. "If you knew that why did you need me?"

"I didn't know that," I said. "I surmised."

"That was a hell of a surmise. We could use someone like you at HUD. Too bad you keep such strange hours."

"Thanks, Chad. I owe you one."

"Or two; I've lost track."

# 27.

It was 6:30 p.m., and the kids were playing at a neighbor's house.

I was in my study going over my notes and reviewing the internet video feed of Kingsley's shooting. Despite myself I laughed as I watched Kingsley ducking and dodging the bullets. Although immortal, each shot must have hurt like hell, and, at the time, the bullets had done serious enough damage to render him almost useless.

I paused on the clearest image of the shooter, which was still pretty grainy. Unfortunately, due to the poor quality of the image, it was impossible to tell if the shooter had been Rick Horton. Whoever it had been was wearing a generic warm-up jacket and a red ball cap. Seemed obvious to me that the shooter was wearing a fake mustache, too, but I couldn't be sure. It just seemed too prominent, and in one frame it even stuck out at an odd angle, as if the glue had come undone. This, too, was noted in the police file.

I now knew Horton owned a .22, and a .22 was used in the crime. Where did that get me? Not much, but at least it was a start.

I felt uneasy, unrested, *undead*.

Shrugging my shoulders, which at this time of the day suddenly seemed twice as heavy, I absently rubbed—or sought—an ache in my neck that seemed always to move just beyond my fingertips. Like trying to catch a fish with your bare hands. Since my attack, since my change, my body ached in places and in ways I had never thought possible.

*Maybe this is what it feels like to be dead.*

I next found an article on the internet about the murder of Hewlett Jackson, Kingsley's one-time client who had taken nine shots to the face. And, not being a werewolf, he promptly died. Hewlett's body had been found in a parking lot, still inside his car, shot outside a seedy bar I was unfortunately familiar with. There had been no robbery, just a blatant killing.

Interestingly, no one yet had made a connection with Jackson's murder to Kingsley's attack.

Maybe I was barking up the wrong tree.

*Did werewolves bark?*

I sat back in my chair and stared up at the painted ceiling. The cobwebs in one corner of the room were swaying gently, though I felt no breeze. I should probably clean those someday. The sun was due to set in a few minutes. Its lingering presence in the sky was the reason behind my current uneasiness and shortness of breath and general foul temperament.

I used to worship the sun. Now it was my enemy.

Or, like Superman, my kryptonite.

I drummed my short fingers on the desk. My nails were thick and somewhat pointed. The nails themselves were impossible to cut. They shaped themselves and seemed to hold steady at that length.

I wondered again if Horton had hired a killer.

But that didn't feel right. No hitman worth his salt would have made such a blatant and dangerous attempt in broad daylight. In front of video cameras. In front of a goddamn courthouse. No. The shooter was making a point; most important, the shooter had not cared about getting caught. I was sure of that. Oh, he cared just enough to wear some silly disguise, but I truly felt in my heart that the shooter had not expected to actually escape.

But they had.

There was a knock on my front door. I swung my feet around and stood. My legs were a little shaky. The shakiness was due to the lingering presence of the sun. I moved slowly through the house, to the front door.

And standing there in my doorway was Detective Sherbet of the Fullerton Police Department. He was holding a bag of donuts.

# 28.

We sat in the living room.

I was in my grandmother's rocking chair and he was in the sofa across from me. The sun was still minutes from setting, and I felt vulnerable. My mind was firing at a slower rate. My body was sluggish. In fact, I felt mortal. I forced myself to focus on the detective sitting before me.

Sherbet held out the bag of donuts. "Place on Orangethorpe makes them fresh this time everyday."

I glanced inside the open bag and my stomach turned. "You are perpetuating the stereotype of policemen and donuts," I said.

"Hell, I *am* the reason for that stereotype." He chuckled to himself. "Lord knows how many of these I've eaten. Can't be too bad for you. I'm sixty-seven and still going strong."

I looked away when he took a healthy bite into his donut.

"You don't look too well, Mrs. Moon. Is it too early in the day for you? I tried coming when the sun set, you know, with your skin condition and all. Now what sort of condition do you have?"

I told him.

"Yeah, right, that one," he said. "Well, I looked into it."

"Really?"

"Oh, I'm not trying to snoop on you, Mrs. Moon, I assure you. I just love learning new things. Always been that way."

I nodded; he was snooping on me.

He continued, "Anyway, apparently it's a very rare condition. Usually shows up first in children, not so much in adults...." He let his voice trail off.

"Well, I'm a late bloomer. Always been that way." I wasn't feeling too chatty. Warning bells were sounding in my head—only my head felt too dull to sort through them. "What can I do for you, detective?"

"Oh, just wondering how your case is coming along. Actually, *our* case is coming along." He chuckled again.

"Our case is moving along fine," I said.

"Any leads?"

"Not yet." I'm always hesitant to share any information to cops. At least, not until I'm ready. When I needed Sherbet, I'd come to him. Not the other way around.

He finished the donut and licked his fingers; he fished around in the bag—which must have gotten his fingers sticky all over again—and removed a cinnamon cake. He seemed pleased with his selection and promptly took a healthy bite.

I was sucking air carefully. My lungs felt somehow smaller. I was having a hell of a hard time getting a decent breath.

His eyes flicked over at me. "You okay, Mrs. Moon?"

"Yes; it's just a little bright for me."

"Your shades are down. We are practically sitting in the dark."

I motioned toward the weak sunlight peaking through a crack in the curtains. "Any sunlight at all can be harmful."

"You have a sensitive condition."

"Very."

"There was a murder in Fullerton a week ago," he said, biting into the cinnamon donut. He wasn't looking at me. "Kid was drained of his blood, or at least most of it. The thing is, the medical examiner doesn't know where the blood went."

"What do you mean?"

"I mean the kid was lying there on the sidewalk, shot to death, and there wasn't an ounce of blood around him—or even in him, for that matter." This time he didn't chuckle.

"Maybe he, you know, bled elsewhere."

"Maybe." Sherbet took another sizable bite. Cinnamon drifted down, glittering in the angled sunlight coming in through the blinds. "No one knows who shot him. No one heard anything. So I keep at it. You know, just doing my job. I find out that the victim is a known banger, has a long rap sheet, name of Gilberto. I talk to Gilberto's friends, discover they had a party the night of his murder. But that's all I get from them. I figure the victim must have been shot after their little party." He paused. "And then we find this."

The detective licked his fingers and reached inside his Members Only jacket and pulled out a photograph of a hand gun. "Kids found it in the bushes a few streets down the road. We test the gun, discover it's the same gun that did the banger. We also lift some prints from it. Turns out the prints belong to Gilberto's uncle. Guy's name is Elias. So I shake down Elias the other night, and he says he shot the gun in self-defense."

Detective Sherbet peered inside the donut bag carefully. The room was still and quiet. Sherbet's face was half-hidden in shadows. The bag crinkled as his hand groped for the next donut. "So I push Elias some more, really come down on him. Believe it or not, I can be a real hardass if I want to be."

Actually, I believed it.

He continued. "And he tells me the whole story. I follow up on the story with the others who were there that night. The story checks out." He paused and studied me carefully. The whites of his eyes shone brightly in the dark. His wide was was hard and still. "The story goes like this. They were partying. A woman shows up. Jogging, believe it or not, in the dead of night. Anyway, I get a teenage punk to admit that they were going to gang rape her. But things go wrong, horribly wrong."

I said nothing.

"Turns out they cornered a tigress." He chuckled softly and went to town on a chocolate old fashioned. He worked his way along the outer rim of the donut. "She showed them hell. A real G.I. Jane."

I almost laughed. I wasn't quite sure what that meant, but it sounded funny.

He continued. "She apparently picks this Gilberto scumbag up by the throat. A two hundred and fifty pound man. Picks him up with one hand. And that's when the story gets a little fuzzy. At some point around that time a gun goes off, and Gilberto takes a bullet in the chest. The others flee like the scattering rats they are. One of them, hiding in the bushes, watches the woman carry off Gilberto's corpse into the dead of night."

We were silent. I could almost hear his tired digestive system going to work on the donuts.

"Hell of a campfire story, if you ask me," he said. He wadded up the paper bag. "What do you think about all of that?"

"Hard to believe."

He chuckled. "Exactly. Group of guys out having fun, drunk and fist-fighting and things turn ugly and a gun goes off, and one of them turns up dead. Happens all of the time. Sometimes the group will even put their heads together and come up with a wild story."

He held the wadded-up donut bag in both hands. He rested his chin on top of his hands and stared at me. "But I ain't ever heard of a story more wild than this."

I continued saying nothing.

"You ever jog alone at night, Mrs. Moon?"

"Yes."

We sat quietly. "Now, as far as I can tell, this girl committed no crime. She was acting in self-defense, and I can guarantee you she taught these boys a lesson. I've never seen a group of men so fucking spooked in my life. Still, I would kind of like to know what she did with that body. I mean it went missing for a few hours, then reappeared later that morning. Minus a lot of blood. You have any thoughts on that, Mrs. Moon?"

"No, I'm sorry."

He stood up and gave me his card. "Well, thanks for chatting with an old man. I expect to see more of you."

"Lucky you."

He stepped over to the front door. "Oh, and Mrs. Moon...were you jogging that night?"

"Which night was that?"

He told me.

"Yes," I said.

"And you didn't see anything?"

"Nothing that would help you, detective."

"Great, thank you."

He shook my hand, holding it carefully in both of his. His hands were so very warm. He nodded once and then left my home.

*So very warm....*

# 29.

I drove slowly past the massive Gothic home, peering through the wrought iron fortification. The house was dark and still. I continued by the brooding structure, parked around the corner and killed the minivan's engine.

Other than a handful of trash cans mixed between some parked cars, the street was empty, as it should be at 2:00 a.m., the vampire's hour.

Whatever that means.

A small wind scuttled a red Carl's Jr. hamburger wrapper along the gutter. Hamburgers are not on my short list of acceptable foods, although raw hamburger meat has been known to sometimes—sometimes—stay down. Where it went, of course, I had no idea.

New topic.

The brick fence that ran along the east side of Horton's home was almost entirely covered in ivy. Streetlamps were few and far between, and none on this particular corner. Better for me.

I stepped out of the minivan and into the cool night air. The darkness was comforting. Perhaps I needed the darkness more than it needed me, but I liked to think that I enriched and added flavor to the night. I liked to believe I gave the night some purpose, a sort of symbiotic relationship.

It was 2:00 a.m., the vampire's hour, and I was feeling good.

I approached the vine-covered wall and did a cursory look around. No one was out. The street was empty. The wall before me was ten feet high and topped with iron spikes. Spikes, stakes, ice picks, railroad spikes, of course, all made me nervous. Hell, I've been known to shudder at the sight of a toothpick.

With a small crowbar tucked into a loop on my jeans, I paused briefly beneath the brick fence and then jumped. High. Soaring through the air.

I landed on top and grabbed hold of an iron spike in each hand. Early on in my vampirism, I discovered I could dunk a basketball. Basketball rims were typically about ten feet high. The kids at the local park had been impressed beyond words. So was I. We had, of course, been playing at night.

Careful of the iron spikes, I squatted there on top of the wall like an oversized—albeit cute—frog. In true amphibian-like fashion, I jumped over the spikes and landed smoothly on the far side of the wall, hands flat on the cement.

I dashed around to the back of the house, and promptly pulled up short, coming face to face, or face to muzzle, with two startled Doberman pinchers. Both were huge and beautiful, sleek and powerful. Both blended perfectly with the night.

Their surprise at seeing me turned quickly to fear. No doubt they caught a whiff of me. Whimpering, they turned and dashed off. Had they owned tails, those would have been tuck between their hind legs; as it were, their round nubs shuddered like frightened little moles poking up through the dark earth. The dogs disappeared within some thick shrubbery near a tool shed.

I had that effect on dogs, and animals in general, who seem to sort of see right through my human disguise. I guess they didn't like what they saw. Too bad. I love dogs.

Horton's house might have an alarm. Hell, in Southern California many lesser homes had some form of security. Although I suspected the Dobermans were the extent of the backyard security, I wasn't taking any chances with the downstairs French doors. Instead, I focused on the second floor balcony with its sliding glass door, leading, by my reckoning, to a guest bedroom.

I reached up, gripped the edge of the balcony's wooden floor. In one fluid motion, I pulled myself up and over the railing and landed squarely in the center of the balcony, which shuddered slightly. Next, I used the pry bar to jimmy open the sliding glass door's lock. Luckily, nothing broke. This time. I was getting better at this.

I stepped into the house.

# 30.

It was indeed the guest room.

The bed, however, was currently empty of guests. A massive Peruvian tapestry hung behind the bed, evoking a simple scene of village life. Moonlight shone through the open drapes, splashing silver over everything. I loved moonlight. Sunlight was overrated.

The air was musky. Newly-stirred dust motes drifted into the moonbeams. Being a trained investigator, I surmised this room hadn't been used in quite some time.

I stepped through into a dark hallway. Well, dark for others, that is. For me, the hallway crackled with molten streams of quicksilver energy, turning everything into distinct shades of gray. Better than any flashlight.

The hallway segued into a wooden railing. Beyond, was a view of the downstairs living room.

And that's when I met the Cat From Hell.

It was sitting on the railing in perfect repose, forepaws together, tail swishing, ears back, its reflective yellow eyes bright spheres of hate. It growled from deep within its chest cavity; we stared at each other for about twenty seconds, just two creatures of the night crossing paths.

Apparently, it wasn't feeling the same sort of kinship.

Like an umbrella, its fur sprang open. Pop. Then it *screeched* bloody hell, and in one quick movement, slashed me across my face. It leaped from the railing, darted down the hallway, hung a right and disappeared down a flight of stairs.

I touched my cheek. The little shit. The wound was already scabbing. I knew within minutes it would be gone altogether.

Still. The little shit.

I waited motionless, certain someone would come to investigate the devil cat. But no one came.

I continued on, and at end of the hall I peaked into an open door. There, sleeping as peaceful as can be, was Rick Horton. From the doorway, I studied his massive room and noted the various antique furnishings, especially the massive, ornate mirror. The room itself was immaculate; everything in its place. Because of that, it was the last place I would have wanted to sleep. A bedroom needed to be lived in.

Rick Horton slept on an undraped four-poster bed. Instead, coats, sweaters and slacks hung neatly from hangers along the horizontal canopy board, perhaps an extension of his closet. Beneath the bed was a cardboard box. The box was slightly askew and not in accordance with the rigorous precision of the room, as if it had been recently shoved under the bed.

I walked quietly to his bedside. Little did Horton realize that an honest-to-God vampire was leaning over him in his sleep, peering down at the smooth slope of his pale neck, where a fat vein pulsed invitingly. I could easily overpower him, tear open the flesh and start drinking. It would be so easy, and warm blood tasted... *so... goddamn... good.*

I sighed and turned my attention to the box, sliding it silently from beneath the bed. Horton never stirred, although I wondered if his sub-conscious was somehow aware of me. Perhaps at this very moment he was fleeing a beautiful vampire in his dreams. Okay, maybe not beautiful, but certainly damn cute with a curvy little body. I wondered fleetingly if the vampire in his dreams catches him. If so, what does she do with him?

I exited the room and made my way back through the long hallway and found a cavernous study. I didn't risk turning on the light. Instead, I pulled open the curtains and allowed for some moonlight, and sat down in a brass-studded executive chair behind a black lacquer desk. I opened the box.

Inside were folders and papers. I removed the first folder, flipped it open and was greeted almost immediately with my own agency's business card stapled to a sheet of paper. Written on the paper was my physical description. I was pleased to say that I was referred to as being *thin* and *pretty*. There was more. A meticulously written recap of our conversation. Most disturbing was a description of my minivan and my license plate number. He had watched me leave.

The second file was much thicker. Inside was a vast array of facts and photographs of Hewlett Jackson, Kingsley's now-murdered client. Hewlett was a young black man, good-looking. There were some pictures of him coming and going from a residence, pictures of him leaving a white Ford Mustang, of him sitting in a park with a female companion, or him drinking late at night with friends at an outdoor restaurant. Careful notes were made of times and places of Hewlett's movements and activities.

One particular time and place was circled in red ink. Most interesting was that it was the exact time and place Hewlett was found murdered.

The last file contained similar information on Kingsley Fulcrum. I read the entire file with much interest, then closed the box, exited the study and returned the whole shebang back under Horton's bed. I even made sure the box was slightly askew.

I stared down at the man who had lost his brother within this last year. I felt pity for him. But Rick Horton had decided to take justice into his own hands. And that's where my pity ended.

And, according to his notes, I was next on his list.

I could kill him now and never worry that he might make an unwanted appearance with my children present. But I do not kill people, especially people defenseless in their sleep. Better to let the law handle this.

I slipped away into the night.

# 31.

It was early afternoon, and I felt like crap, and I would continue to feel like crap until the sun disappeared in a few hours. We were at Hero's again, where very few people knew our names, but at least the bartender remembered our drinks.

"Two glasses of chardonnay?" he asked, giving us a warm smile. He had cute dimples around his mouth. Thick lips, too. Thick, juicy lips.

"You bet," Mary Lou said, beaming. He winked and moved down the bar to pour our drinks, and Mary Lou continued smiling at his back, or perhaps at his backside. "Isn't he just amazing? What a memory!"

"Down girl. It's his job to remember," I said. "He does well to remember."

He returned with our drinks. Mary Lou handed him her credit card, although she probably would have preferred to slip it inside the waistband of his Jockey shorts. She sipped carefully from her glass and finally looked over at me. "So what's the latest news with your case?"

"Are you done undressing our bartender with your eyes?"

"No yet. Wait. Okay, now I am."

"You're a married woman, with kids," I said.

"I know. Your point?"

"Married women shouldn't be undressing bartenders with their eyes."

"Show me that in the rule book."

"There is no rule book."

She looked at me. "Exactly. Now tell me about your case."

I gave her an update, and to her credit she forgot about the bartender and his buns and focused on me.

"Well, Horton's obviously your guy. What a fucking creep." She shuddered slightly.

"Do you talk this way around your kids?"

"No, just you. I let it all out around you."

"Lucky me," I said.

"And you were next on his list?" she asked.

"You know, to silence the pesky private eye."

"You are kind of pesky, aren't you?"

"The peskier the better."

"So what're you going to do?" she asked.

I sipped some wine. I tasted nothing, literally, but at least I didn't double over with stomach cramps. Sipping from the wine glass gave me some semblance of normalcy. "I'm going to have a talk with Detective Sherbet this evening."

"But what can he do?" asked my sister. "He can't just barge in there and arrest the guy without probable cause."

"You've been watching too much TV, but you're right. Not without a search warrant. And one needs evidence to obtain a search warrant."

"So breaking into this guy's house and finding evidence hidden under his bed won't fly with a judge, right?"

"Right," I said.

"So what will you do?" she asked.

"The detective and I will figure something out."

"Will you tell this detective about your break-in?"

"Yeah, probably."

"Will he like it?"

"Probably not."

We were silent, and I decided now was the time to tell her about the attempted rape and the death of the gang banger—and about the sucking of blood. So I did. The story took a few minutes, during which Mary Lou said nothing although I noted she had quickly finished her drink.

"That was very reckless of you," she said when I was done.

"I know."

"And you really drank his blood?"

"Yes."

She was silent. I was silent. The noises of the bar came floating to my ears, the chink of glasses being washed in the sink, the sound of laughter behind me, the snapping opening of the cash register drawer.

"What if this somehow causes you to lose control, Samantha?"

"I love my kids too much to lose control."

"Then you took a foolish chance by drinking that man's blood."

"Yes, I did. But the situation had gotten quickly out of control. Before I knew it, I was holding a corpse."

"You should not be jogging so late."

I drank my wine. Sometimes Mary Lou was impossible to talk to.

"When is there a better time? I'm a goddamn vampire."

"The early evening."

"In the early evening I have the kids and work."

"Then why do you need to jog at all?"

"Because it helps me stay sane."

We were alone at this end of the counter. As we spoke, my eyes constantly scanned the crowd, making sure we had no eavesdroppers. "I walk a fine line, Mary Lou. Everything around me is threatening to crumble away. Something like exercise is within my control. I need control right now."

"Maybe you need help."

We had gone through this before. "There's no one to help me."

"Maybe you need to speak to a therapist, someone, anyone."

"You think this is in my head?"

"No. It's real. I know that."

"The moment I tell a therapist that I'm a vampire, they'll lock me up and take away my kids. Is that what you want?"

She didn't answer immediately.

"Is that what you want, Mary Lou?"

"No, it's not what I want, but I also think your kids are not living a very healthy and normal life." She sighed and reached out and held my hand. "You are a good mother, I know that. I know your kids mean everything to you, but I think they are in an unhealthy environment."

"I see it as a *different* environment," I said, then studied her concerned face. "Wait. Do you worry for their safety?"

She said nothing.

"Do you worry that I will have a craving and drink from my own children?"

Nothing.

"You do, don't you?"

She sucked in some air. "No, of course not. But if you keep behaving recklessly you might, you know, someday lose sight of who you are. Sam, you've fought for so long to keep things together. I don't want to see your life crumble around you just because you found the taste of one man's blood particular good."

I studied her and she looked away. I suddenly had an insight. "You've been talking to Danny, haven't you?"

She reddened. "Yes. He called me the other night to apologize for not picking up the kids. He's worried about the kids."

"Oh, really? And he shows this by coming home at midnight?"

She shrugged. "He worries that you will have a negative influence on their lives. I told him that was ridiculous. No mother loves her kids more than you."

We were silent. It was just before dusk, and I was irritable and cranky and tired. I wanted to sleep.

"He's screwing someone else," I said.

"You know for sure?"

"No. But I'm going to find out."

"I'm sorry, Sam."

"So am I. But it was bound to happen, right? Who wants to be married to a freak?"

"You're not a freak," she said, and then cracked a smile. "Well, okay, maybe a little freaky."

I laughed. She reached out and took my hand. I reveled in the warmth.

She said, "So what are you going to do, Sam?"

"Follow him," I said. "I am, after all, an ace detective."

# 32.

The sun had just set, and I was in Detective Sherbet's office. I felt good. Most important, I felt cognizant and lucid.

I sat in the visitor's chair in front of his desk and noticed for the first that Sherbet was a handsome man. His arms were heavily muscled and tan, with dark hair circling his forearms. I didn't usually go for arm hair on men, but on Sherbet it seemed fitting and a little exciting. He seemed like a man's man, powerful and virile. No wonder it galled him to think his kid might be gay.

"So how did the basketball game go the other day?" I asked.

There was a greasy bag of donuts sitting on top of a very full trash can. The scent of donut oil was foul, and slightly upsetting to my stomach. I fought through it.

"Kid was horrible. He actually took a shot at the wrong basket. Hell, he almost even made it. I nearly cheered. The coach benched him after that."

"Did your boy have fun?"

"No. He was miserable."

"Did you have fun?"

"No. I was embarrassed."

"So what are you going to do? Keep forcing him to play?"

"You sound like my wife."

"Your wife sounds like she might be the only reasonable parent in your household."

"I don't know what I'm going to do with that kid."

"Just love him."

"I do."

Our section of the police station was empty and quiet. The detective had his hands clasped over his rotund belly. Although his stomach could have been flatter, the roundness sort of added to his manhood, pronouncing him as a real man who wasn't afraid to eat.

"You're looking at my fat belly," he said.

"I would call it rotund," I said.

"Rotund? Are you trying to get on my good side?"

"Maybe."

He rubbed a hand over the curving sweep of his belly, then played with one of the clear plastic buttons. His face turned somber. "Samantha, I know you were assaulted six years ago, here in Fullerton. It's in your record. You were found in Hillcrest Park, half-dead. Your throat torn open. Although there was little blood at the scene, you had almost bled to death. At first it was believed that you might have been attacked by an animal, a dog or coyote. But later you told investigators that it had been a man. He was never found."

"Detective, I don't want to talk about—"

"Now, I understand you might not want to talk about it, but there's something strange going on here in my town, my backyard, so to speak. My beat. I would appreciate if maybe someday you could help me understand."

"Someday," I said. "Just not today."

"Okay, fine. On to item number two. What do you have on the Fulcrum case?"

Relieved to be talking about anything else, I told him everything I knew about Horton. When I got to the part about breaking and entering Horton's home, I said, "Are you going to arrest me?"

"Not yet. Keep going."

"Horton had files on Hewitt Jackson and Kingsley Fulcrum, not to mention a new file on me. In these files are detailed information on Jackson's and Fulcrum's movements. A date and time was circled on Jackson. In fact, it was the exact date and time he was murdered."

Detective Sherbet's eyes widened a little. For Sherbet, this was the next best thing to him jumping up and down and yelling *yippee!* "Then he's our man."

"Yes, I think so."

"You think so? Hell, he had everything but the smoking gun. And he might still have that, as well, once we serve a search warrant."

"He just doesn't feel right."

"Is that your gut talking?"

"Yes."

"Well, my gut says he's our man."

"How are you going to convince a judge to issue a warrant?"

He sat back, laced his fingers behind his thick head of salt and pepper hair. "Good question. Any ideas?"

"You're the homicide detective."

He thought about that. "How about a trash run?"

"As in dig through his trash?" I said.

"Sure. It's public domain. We find something incriminating we can convince a judge to issue a warrant."

I blinked. "We?"

"Yes, I'm not going to dig through his trash alone."

"The trash went out last night," I said. "I saw the barrels."

"It's settled then. Next Thursday we go out to Horton's place and dig through his trash."

"Sounds like a date."

"Let's just hope we find something."

"Oh, I'm sure we'll find something," I said. "Let's just hope we find the *right* something."

# 33.

The kids were in karate class together, so I used the opportunity to work-out at Jacky's. It was late evening, and the sun had set. I was feeling strong and healthy. At the moment, Jacky was taping my fists. We were both silent. I think he sensed I was in one of my moods. Occasionally, he would look up into my face, then quickly avert his eyes.

"I'm not going to bite you, Jacky."

"You think I'm afraid of you?" he asked. "Well, I am."

I rubbed his shining head with my already-taped right hand.

In fact, I was having a hard time letting go of my conversation with Mary Lou. I was trying to comprehend the fact that she had been secretly speaking to Danny. Discussing what an unfit mother I was.

"Whatever's eating at you," said Jacky, "take it out on the punching bag. That's my motto."

And so I did. Pummeling the thing until I was dripping sweat. We worked in three minute drills, with Jacky screaming at me to keep my hands up. I would finish each round in a flurry of punches, rapid-fire body shots to the punching bag. During one of these flurries, I caught Jacky's expression as he steadied the punching bag. It was one of profound pain. The punches were reverberating through the bag and into him. The Irishman was taking a beating, but he seemed to love it.

At the end of the sixth round I dropped my hands to my side. The gloves felt like bags of cement. Jacky staggered away to get some water.

I leaned my forehead against the punching bag. I was still thinking about Danny. It seemed to me that he was building a case against me. Of course, building a case against me couldn't be easier. Hell, in my current condition, even I knew I was an unfit mother. But I was doing my best and I loved my kids with all my heart. You could never replace that. Ever.

At the far end of the gym, I noticed a tall boxer working out with one of Jacky's long-time trainers. The boxer was young and blond and very muscular. His punches were rapid and precision-like. His muscles stood out on his hot skin.

Jacky came back, holding a little Dixie cup full of water. The cup was shaking in his hands.

"I've been meaning to talk to you about those Dixie cups," I said. "We pay good money to join your gym, and the best you can give us are these paper thimbles in return?"

"Ah, lass, you pay for the atmosphere."

I nodded toward the young, hot shot boxer. "Who's that?"

"That's Desmond Beacon. A boxing champion in the Marines, went undefeated. He's turning pro."

"I want to box him."

Jacky's eyes brightened briefly—perhaps with excitement—and then he came back down to earth and shook his head. "Look, kid, I know I built your hopes up and all that, but that ain't going to happen. Maybe we could arrange a fight with another broad."

"Broad?" I said. "Maybe I should box *you*." I looked again at the ex-Marine. "I want to fight *him*."

"No, lass. I'm sorry."

"So he kicks my ass. At least it'll give me something else to think about."

Jacky looked at me and sighed. "Your day that shitty, huh?"

I thought of Danny cheating—or possibly cheating—and I thought of possibly losing my kids. "Yeah," I said. "Hell of a shitty day."

He sighed again and said, "Hold on." He went over to the Wonder Kid and his trainer, spoke briefly, pointed at yours truly. Desmond Beacon shook his head, said something, and they all laughed. All of them, that is, except Jacky. He got into the tall Marine's face. By got into his face, I mean, Jacky looked up from the man's chest. I had no doubt that Jacky could have taken the Marine in his day. But his day was long past him. They stared each other down for another ten seconds and then the Marine turned away, dismissing Jacky with a contemptuous smirk.

"What was that all about?" I asked when Jacky had hobbled back.

"Fucking prick," said Jacky. "I have a mind to kick his ass."

"What did he say?"

"Doesn't matter."

"He doesn't want to fight me?"

"Doesn't matter."

"It's because I'm a woman."

"He said something about that," said Jacky, looking back at the Marine, who had gone back to shadow boxing. "Actually, he said something about doing something else to you, but I ain't gonna repeat it to you."

"Is that when you stuck up for me?"

"The kid's disrespectful. Someone needs to show him a lesson."

"I agree."

"Samantha...I get nervous when I see that look in your eye."

But I wasn't listening. I was already marching over to the six foot four Desmond Beacon, who was shadow boxing near the ring. When he saw me coming he stopped, nudged his trainer, and grinned. A wolfish sort of grin. When I got to him, I looked him in the eye, smiled sweetly, and promptly kicked him square in the balls.

*Hope he's wearing a cup.*

His eyes bulged and a look of confusion swept across his face and then he dropped to a knee, groaning and turning red.

*Guess not.*

His little trainer shrieked like a monkey. He grabbed my shoulder and tried flinging me around, but I don't fling easily and he lost his balance. Instead, he settled for getting in my face. "What the hell are you doing, Missy? Are you out of your goddamn mind?"

"Just maybe," I said. I pushed the trainer aside and looked down at the boxer kneeling before me. I felt like a queen. "Will you fight me now?"

Desmond Beacon looked up. His face had gone from red to green.

"You bet your ass," he croaked.

# 34.

Jacky and I were in a corner of the ring.

The little Irishman was doing some last minute adjustments to my head gear. The headgear felt big and clunky. I didn't think I needed it, but having it on seemed to make the others happy. The Marine, in the opposite corner, was also wearing head gear. I assumed he, too, felt the gear was unnecessary.

I stared down at Jacky's bald head as he now worked on my gloves. From this angle I could just make out some old boxing scars above his brow. Many, many old boxing scars. There was a wicked little gleam in Jacky's eye whenever he looked up at me; he was breathing hard and fast, face red with excitement.

"Remember what I always tell you," he said, "keep your gloves up."

"Keep them up? Or down? I get confused."

But Jacky wasn't listening. In fact, he had this sort of dreamy look on his face. Perhaps he had regressed back to the backroom fighting halls of 1950's Belfast, when he was a young prize fighter with something to prove. His fighting days were long gone and I had a feeling I was his outlet, but that was okay. I wanted to fight. I wanted an honest-to-God slugfest. Sometimes you just need to beat the crap out of something.

"Focus on your jabs, doll."

"Don't call me doll, and I'll focus on whatever I want. This isn't a real fight. I'm just going to beat the crap out of him and then pick up my kids."

Jacky pushed me away and held me at arm's length. "Don't get too cocky, kid. You're strong as hell, and to be honest, a little freaky, but this guy knows the fundamentals. I'm not sure you realize what the hell you've gotten yourself into."

"We'll see."

Jacky held up a white towel. "I'm throwing this in if things turn ugly."

"For me or him?"

"Either."

* * *

"Ding ding," said Jacky.

Desmond Beacon stood nearly a foot taller than me. In the center of the ring we touched gloves. Now that the pain was gone from his groin, he didn't look so eager to fight a woman—especially now that we had a few female onlookers.

So, to get him back into the spirit of things, I hit him with a quick jab that landed on his chin and snapped his head back. When his head settled back into place, there was a suitable look of irritation in his eyes.

Behind me, Jacky screamed, "Yes, yes!"

Desmond now bounced on his toes and worked his neck, and suddenly flicked his glove out at me much quicker than I was prepared for. I tried to dodge right, but there was no escaping it. His glove hit me square in the jaw and I staggered backwards and promptly landed on my ass, skidding to a halt near the ropes.

"Sammy, you okay?" Jacky's worried, ruddy face peered down at me through the lowest rung of rope.

I got up. "I'm fine."

"I don't like this, Sammy. He's too good."

"Don't call me Sammy."

"Then what the hell do you want me to call you?"

"Just Sam."

We touched gloves again. Desmond wasn't smiling. In fact, he didn't seem to be enjoying any of this. I think he was hoping I would've gone away by now. We circled each other. I was wary of his hand speed. His face was expressionless, although his cheeks were pinched together because of the headgear. He kept his gloves up like a good boy. His fist shot out again, another jab. I blocked it with my own glove, but the force of the punch knocked my own glove back into my forehead. Luckily the head gear is thickest at the forehead. He jabbed again. I blocked it and side-stepped. He was waiting for me to side-step. His next punch rung my bell, and I staggered backward again.

I caught a glimpse of Jacky. Or, rather, *two* Jackys. The old Irishman looked stricken. His interest in seeing a real fight had long ago dissipated. He was holding the white towel up. I shook my head at him, and he reluctantly lowered it.

Back in the ring, Desmond looked a little surprised to see me still on my feet. We circled each other some more. It seemed apparent to me that the Marine and his manager, and perhaps even Jacky, had agreed that I would only receive jabs. Harmless enough, and not too brutal.

Wouldn't bode well for Jacky's female clientèle to watch a woman get pulverized by a semi-professional male boxer.

Now even more people were watching. A small crowd of mostly women were standing around the sparring ring, all dripping sweat, their workouts finished or abandoned. They were talking amongst themselves and watching me closely. I didn't like close scrutiny, but I needed to pound something, and the Marine was the biggest thing in the gym.

I focused entirely on the Marine. Sweat dripped steadily down his cheeks and into his headgear. The muscles in his right shoulder flexed and I took a step back just as his lightning-fast jab swished through the air. *Focus on the shoulder.* The deltoid muscles flinched again and I moved back again and avoided the next punch as well. We circled, and he stopped bouncing on his feet and lowered his hands. The moment he lowered his hands, I delivered a combination of left jab and overhead right. Both landed. I am quick when I want to be and strong when I want to be, and I wanted to be both now. The punches staggered him backward and he landed against the ropes. A chorus of cheers erupted from the milling crowd of sweating women. The Marine pushed himself off the ropes and approached me, fists raised. He was looking at the crowd of women out of the corner of his eye. He didn't know what to do. He was in a hell of spot. He didn't want to hurt a woman, yet here was a woman in front of him who was hurting him. I decided to make that decision for him, and came at him like a bull. I faked a left jab and then came hard over his gloves with a straight right that hit him square on the nose. His knees buckled. I hit him again. He gathered himself and quit looking at the crowd. Good. Now he danced around the ring like he meant it. Good. He lifted his gloves and delivered a powerful combination that I used my gloves and arms to absorb. His punches hurt. He was throwing them hard. He didn't give a damn who was watching him now or how bad this might have looked. He was tired of some woman taking potshots at him.

Except I wasn't *some woman.*

Even with the sun still out in the late afternoon sky, my reflexes were better than average. But only slightly better. I still felt weak and sluggish—and that damn sun couldn't set fast enough.

The Marine suddenly threw a wild punch that veered off my shoulder and I used that opening to deliver a rocking uppercut. I caught him under the chin and his head snapped up. He might have even lifted off the mat. Either way, he landed hard on his back. The crowd went wild. Alright, maybe not wild, but definitely a few cheers. The Marine got up and we touched gloves in the middle of the ring again. His eyes seemed a little unsteady. The big boy had taken a few hard blows to the head from a very healthy vampire. He raised his fists, did a little boxing dance, and sort of refocused himself.

And came out swinging.

Holy crap! Hell hath no fury like a man embarrassed by a woman. His punches were powerful and numerous; some landed, but most missed entirely. I soon found myself backed up against the ropes. Spit and sweat and blood flung from the Marine. His arms were a blur of punches. I heard gasps behind me. Surely this looked horrible to Jacky's female clientèle: a woman being beaten to a pulp by a hulking Marine. I'm sure Jacky was about to throw in the towel, when it happened.

I didn't see it happen, granted.

But I *felt* it.

The late afternoon soon had finally set, and I felt alive.

*So damn alive.*

I slipped under his onslaught and backed into a corner. He was about to follow me in but must have seen something in my eyes and paused. He should have kept pausing. Instead, he charged ahead. As he came at me, I timed my punch perfectly. A hard right to the jaw.

*Too hard.*

Never had I hit something so squarely and so hard. I floored him. No. I lifted him off his feet and over the surrounding ropes. He landed in a heap on the padded floor. Women screamed and rushed over to him. I saw Jacky run over to the Marine, too. He looked at me, horror on his face.

*What had I done?*

I stood dumbly in the center of the ring as the Marine lay on his back, unmoving.

# 35.

*I almost killed a man today.*

*Tell me about it.*

So I wrote it up for Fang. As usual, he read like a demon on crack, and posted his reply almost instantly.

*The Marine might be re-thinking his boxing career.*

I suddenly felt indignant, perhaps to mask my guilt. *Good. He was a pig, and boxing's certainly no way to make a living. Getting your brains beaten to a pulp day in and day out.*

*I see, so by knocking him out of the ring, you actually did a service to him.*

*Yes. He could think of it as career counseling.*

*Through the school of hard knocks.*

*Haha.*

*I think you are trying to assuage your guilt, Moon Dance, to justify your actions.*

*Okay, fine. I feel horrible! You happy?*

*No. At least you can admit your guilt.*

*He didn't deserve what I did to him.*

*Probably not. Then again, he sounded like he might have needed to be taught a lesson. Did you really kick him in the balls?*

*Argh! I'm horrible!*

# Moon Dance

*Yes,* wrote Fang. *You were today.*
*You don't let me off easy, do you?*
*Do you want me to let you off easy?*

*No,* I wrote, thinking about it. *I want you to always be dead honest with me. It's why I keep you around.*

*Gee, thanks. So what happened to the Marine?*

*They took him away in an ambulance. The paramedic said it looked like a concussion. I sent him flowers and a card apologizing.*

*Perhaps you should find other outlets for your anger,* wrote Fang.

*Perhaps.*

*You might have to be a little more, um, discreet with your gifts. You don't want to keep attracting unwanted attention.*

*I think you're right.* I paused. *But why call it a gift, Fang?*

*It's how you choose to view it, Moon Dance. You could focus on either the negative or the positive. As in all of life.*

*Thank you, Tony Robbins.*

*No, I'm not Tony Robbins but I'm certainly as tall.*

*Really? What else do you look like?* I wrote, eager for more information.

As usual, he ignored any personal questions. *Let's take a look at these gifts of yours. You have enhanced strength, night vision, speed and endurance. Not to mention the ability to shape-change.*

*Whoa!* I wrote, sitting back. *No one's ever said anything about shape-changing.*

*You've never shape-changed, Moon Dance?*

*Ever recall me mentioning turning into a bat?*

There was a long pause, then he wrote: *Most texts, resources and personal accounts are unanimous about this.*

*You should be able to shape-change.  Into what exactly, is open to debate.*

I found myself laughing at my computer desk.  *Well, if your resources can tell me* how *to shape-change, then I'll give it a shot.*

*I'll look into it.  Maybe you should look into it, too.*

*How?*

Another pause: *Maybe you need to look into yourself.*

The doorbell rang.  The babysitter was here.

*Goodnight, Fang.*

*Goodnight, Moon Dance.*

# 36.

It was late and I was restless.

Earlier in the day, I'd dreamed of Kingsley again, and now I couldn't get the big son-of-a-bitch out of my thoughts. In my dream, we were in the woods again, but this time we weren't playing a game. This time he had captured me early on and I was on my back. I distinctly remembered the pine needles poking into my bare back and the sound of small animals scurrying away in the woods. Scurrying away in *fear*. Kingsley was in his half man/half wolf mode, dark shaggy hair hanging from his huge shoulders, down his long arms. A tuft of it sticking up along the ridge of his spine like a hairy stegosaurus. He was on all fours and he was above me. I was pinned beneath him, distinctly aware that he was far too strong for me to push off. I was submitting to him. Body and soul.

In my dream, he was still wearing the medallion, hanging freely from his thick neck, suspended just inches above my face. Whenever I opened my mouth to ask about the medallion, he simply shook his great head and I knew I was not to discuss it, and so I didn't, although I wanted to. Badly.

Then he lowered his face to mine, a face that was still magnificently human and handsome, although in bad need of a shave. His breath was hot on my neck, my ears, through my hair. He was touching me with his lips or tongue, I didn't know which, nor did I care. All I knew is that was I had not felt this good in a long, long time.

Then the alarm went off, and I could have cried.

*A hell of a dream,* I thought. *I think you might like the big guy.*

Ya think?

The question was: what did I do about it? I didn't know. Even though I knew in my heart my marriage was over, I still felt guilty for having feelings for another man.

*You shouldn't. Your husband is long gone. You can't keep living like this, and nor can he.*

But the moment I quit living like this—the moment my husband and I officially separated—would be the moment my kids are taken away from me, and I can't have that.

*I can't have that.*

*So quit thinking about Kingsley.*

Easier said than done.

It was late, and I was restless and I couldn't for the life of me keep Kingsley out of my thoughts. Damn him. What right did he have kissing a lonely and hurting woman? What right did he have of putting me through this?

I nearly laughed. It had, of course, been just a dream.

# 37.

"You home?" I asked.

"Of course I'm home," said Kingsley, "it's two-thirty in the goddamn morning."

"Don't sound so dramatic."

"Dramatic? If anything I sound tired."

"I'm coming over. Where do you live?"

There was a long pause. I wondered if Kingsley had fallen back to sleep. Then a thought occurred to me, maybe he had a woman with him. If so, I didn't care. I wanted to talk, and not with a mortal. Either way, last night had been the full moon, so tonight Kingsley should be his old self.

"Okay," he said, and gave me directions. "Oh, and remind me when you get here that there's something I need to talk to you about."

"That makes two of us."

Kingsley lived in Yorba Linda, just a few cities over. At a quarter to three, I drove east down Bastanchury Blvd. The night was still and quiet. To my left were empty rolling hills. Beyond was the county dump, well hidden from curious eyes and sensitive noses.

Here on Bastanchury were some of the best Orange County had to offer. Beautiful homes slightly removed from the hustle and bustle of the county.

# Moon Dance

I turned left into a long driveway, drove through a tangle of shrubbery along a crushed seashell drive. The seashell drive, reflecting the near full moon, was as bright as a yellow brick road to my eyes. The driveway continued for perhaps an eighth of a mile, until it curved before a massive estate house.

I parked in front of the portico, and briefly admired the huge structure. It was a Colonial revival, complete with two flanker structures on either end. Nearly the entire facade was covered in dark clapboard, and the windows were enclosed with paneled shutters. All in all, a fitting home for a werewolf.

Shortly after I rang the bell, a porch light turned on and a very tall and dour man appeared at the door, who looked down at me from a hawkish nose. He was frowning. Probably wasn't in his job description to be receiving guests at 3:00 a.m. There was something disjointed and odd about the man. It took me a second to realize what it was. One ear was clearly larger than the other.

"This way," he said. "Master Kingsley is waiting in the conservatory."

"With Professor Plum and the candlestick?" I asked.

Big Ear was not amused.

# 38.

Kingsley was lounging on a leather sofa with a drink in hand.

He looked like hell: scruffy beard, hair in disarray, serious bags under his eyes.

"Um, you look good," I said.

"Like hell I do."

"Just what I was thinking."

The conservatory was octagon-shaped and faced the expansive backyard which spread out into the hills beyond like a vast estate. Through the French window, I could make out an alabaster fountain gurgling away, depicting a naked nymph blowing water through her cupped hands. The sculptor went a little crazy with her breasts. Men and breasts. Sheesh.

"Would you like a drink?" Kingsley asked.

"Sure. I'll have whatever you're having."

Kingsley motioned to his butler. A moment later, a drink appeared before me.

"Thank you, Jeeves," I said.

Kingsley grinned. "His name is Franklin."

"Franklin the butler?"

"Yes."

"Doesn't have quite the same ring."

"No, it doesn't," Kingsley said, "but he's a good butler, and can pour a hell of a drink."

"It's true," said Franklin. "I almost never spill." His enunciation was clear and precise with a slightly lilting accent that could have been English. When he spoke, his face appeared completely still, as if the muscles were inert, or de-activated. I couldn't help but notice an ugly scar that ran along his chin and extended back to his hairline, as if Franklin had at one time or another lost his entire head.

Kingsley said, "Thank you, Franklin. That will be all. Sorry to rouse you out of your sleep in the dead of night."

"I am made to serve."

"And you do it so well. Off you go. Good night."

Franklin the Butler nodded and left. Curious, I watched him go. His strides were long and loping, as if his legs were disproportionate to his body.

"Franklin is an interesting fellow," I said when he was gone.

"You don't know the half of it."

"Must have survived a hell of an accident, scarred like that."

"Yeah, something like that."

"Where did you find him?"

"He was recommended by a friend."

I sipped the alcohol. It had no flavor at all, and no effect. The ice rattled in the tumbler.

"What do you know of vampire shape-shifting?" I asked suddenly.

Kingsley blinked, then thought about it. "Not a whole hell of a lot, I'm afraid. Why?"

"It's been coming up lately."

"I see."

"So, *can* vampires turn into, you know, *things*?"

He laughed, "They can indeed turn into...*things*."

My heart slammed in my chest. "What sort of things?" I asked.

"You really don't know, do you?"

"Would I be asking if I did?"

"And you've never tried shape-changing?"

"I wouldn't know where to begin."

"You could always try jumping off a tree branch and see what happens."

"And think like a fruit bat?"

"Is that the gay bat?"

"You're not helping."

"That's just it. I don't know how to help. My own transformation sort of takes place uninvitingly."

"I understand. So back to the question: what sort of things can vampires turn into?"

"Vampires turn into...something big and black." He paused and grimaced as if he had just bitten into something sour. "Something ugly and hideous. Something with massive leathery wings. A sort of hybrid between man and bat."

"You've seen one?"

He hesitated. "Yes."

"And?"

"And that's all I know."

"Who was the vampire?"

"I'd rather not discuss it right now."

"Why?"

He inhaled. His handsome face was mostly hidden in shadows, although that posed little problems for me. I could see the fine lines of his nose and jaw.

"Because he killed my wife."

I breathed. "I'm sorry, Kingsley."

"Hey, it's in the past."

"I ask too many questions. It's the investigator in me. I don't know how to turn it off sometimes."

"You didn't know."

I wanted to ask him more about his wife. Why was she killed? Was she a werewolf, too? If not, then how did they make their marriage work? How long had they been married? And kids? Moreover, who was this vampire? But I held my tongue, which was something I didn't do well. Therefore, I found myself thinking of flying around the city of Fullerton like a super-sized bat out of hell. The image was too crazy. I mean, I'm a mother of two. I went to a PTA meeting last week. I washed twelve loads of laundry over the weekend. Real people don't turn into giant bats, right?

"So basically," I said after a suitable time, "I turn into a monster."

He eased off the sofa and headed to the bar. He poured himself another drink.

"You're not the only one," he said. "Once a month Franklin keeps me locked up in a special room where I won't hurt myself or others." He swirled the contents of his glass. Some of the contents splashed over the rim. He didn't seem to notice or care. "Only monsters need to be locked up."

"But you have taken measures to control the monster within you. In my book, that makes you very much *not* a monster"

"By practicing safe-transformation?" he asked.

I laughed. "Precisely."

As he sat, I noticed a particularly thick tuft of hair at the back of his hand. The hair hadn't been there a few days before. I slipped out of my chair and to his side. I took his hand in my own and ran my fingers through the fur.

"Just what are you doing?" he asked. He didn't move. I could feel his pulse in his wrist. His pulse was quickening. I pulled on the fur.

"It's real," I said.

"Of course it's real."

"You really *are* a werewolf."

"Yes."

"Can I call you Wolfy?

"No."

A glint of amber reflected in his irises. I could have been looking into the eyes of a wolf staring back at me from the deep shadows of a dark forest.

*The forest. My dream. His hot breath. His hotter lips.*

I looked away. God, his stare was hypnotic. No wonder he won so many court cases. What juror could resist those eyes? I noticed then that the couch had a light sprinkling of what appeared to be dog hair. The hair was now on my clothing.

"You're shedding," I said.

"Yes, I tend to do that."

"How old are you Kingsley?"

"You will not be denied tonight, will you, Samantha?"

I shrugged. "Perhaps by understanding more about you, I can understand more about me, about who I am and where I'm going."

"Fine," he said. "I'm seventy-nine."

"Is that in dog years?"

"I'm going to bed," he said.

"Wait. What did you need to talk to me about?"

He nodded solemnly. "There's someone looking for you, Samantha."

"Who?"

"A vampire hunter."

"A...what?"

"A vampire hunter, and he wants you dead."

I choked on my drink. "Why?"

"Because you're a vampire and killing vampires is what he does."

"How does he kill vampires?"

"A crossbow, I think. Apparently arrow bolts have the same affect on vampires as stakes."

"When did you find this out?"

"Tonight."

"How did you find out?"

"I'm privy to such information. Through associates. From others like me."

"Werewolves."

"Yes."

I thought about that, and then told him about the man from the other night with the night-vision goggles. Kingsley shrugged.

"It could have been him. Perhaps he's been following you."

"No one's been following me."

"How do you know?"

"I watch for tails. It's a habit of mine."

"A good habit," he agreed.

"Speaking of tails—"

"I'm going to bed," he said again.

"Wait. What do you propose I do about this vampire hunter?" I asked.

"Kill or be killed. That's where I come in. Let me help you get rid of this guy."

"No," I said. "I'm a big girl and this is my problem."

"He's a trained killer."

"And I've been trained to protect myself."

He didn't like it, but said no more. We sat together on the couch, our shoulders touching.

"Why are you with him, Samantha?"

I knew who he was talking about. Danny. "It's none of your business why."

"Yes," he said, "it is."

"How so?"

"Because I think I'm falling in love with you."

# 39.

It was late.

The kids were with my sister, and I was alone in a parking lot, hidden behind some bushes and beneath an overhanging willow. The digital clock on the car radio read 11:22 p.m. Too late for an attorney and his secretary to be working cases.

The engine was off, and the windows were cracked open. Even vampires need to breathe. Actually, I wondered about that. I held my breath, timing myself. A minute passed. Two minutes. Three. Four. Five. I let out my breath. Well, hell. You learn something new everyday.

Just what dark voodoo was keeping me alive then? Didn't my brain and blood need oxygen, too? Maybe I just didn't need as much, and the only reason I seemed to breathe on a regular basis was that my automatic nervous system didn't know enough to shut off. I felt my heart. It was beating, very slowly. I timed the beating. Ten beats a minute. Ah, hell. I should be dead a hundred times over.

But I wasn't. I was very much alive. But how, dammit?

Maybe it was better not to think about it.

I was alive. Perhaps I should have died six years ago, but I didn't. Something kept me alive, and for that I was thankful. Now, not only could I watch my kids grow up but

I would probably outlive my grandchildren and their children's children.

*Jesus.*

*I ask again: what the hell kind of dark magic is keeping me alive?*

Danny's firm is a small firm. He owned it with a partner, where it occupied the entire second floor of a very plain professional building. Danny specialized in auto accidents. A classic ambulance chaser. He made good money at it, but sold his soul.

I used to give him crap about it long ago, until I realized he actually enjoyed the work. He enjoyed sticking it to the insurance companies. Now he enjoyed sticking it to his secretary.

The night was cool. Trees above me swished gently. The partial moon appeared and disappeared through a smattering of clouds.

There seemed to be a hint of light coming from one of the building's upstairs windows, but it was difficult to tell as the blinds were shut. I sipped from a water bottle. The water was lukewarm. I discovered that I liked lukewarm water, which was a refreshing change from the nightly dosage of chilled hemoglobin.

I thought of the vampire hunter. For the past few days I had been watching my tail, and was confident no one was following me.

Staking out anyone—even your husband—can be boring work. I held up my hand and studied it. My skin was white, almost translucent. Purple veins crisscrossed the back of my hand. My nails were thick and hard. Like my hair, they tended to grow slowly. I touched the center of my palm with my left index finger. The sensation sent a slight shiver up my right arm. Flesh and bone. I was three dimensional. I could feel. I could laugh. I could love my kids.

So why couldn't I die? And what gave me my unnatural strength?

I turned the rearview mirror my direction.

There was nothing in the mirror. Nothing at all, save for an image of the driver's seat headrest. My clothing moved as if occupied by the Invisible Woman. Fairly disconcerting. It was as if the mirror refused to acknowledge my existence. I turned it away in disgust.

"Well, I'm here, dammit," I said to the mirror. "Whether you like it or not."

Or perhaps I was saying this to Danny. Or the world.

So a creature called a vampire had attacked me one night. It tainted my blood with his. Because of that taint I was forever and irrevocably changed.

It had to do with the blood. I thought of blood now. It was the lifesource. Without it, we die. Well, without a lot of other stuff we die, too. Without your head you die. Without your heart you die.

How could something in my blood change me *forever*?

Blood connected everything, flowed through everything. Blood infused throughout the entire body.

The blood, I realized, was the key. My blood, my tainted blood, was keeping my body unnaturally alive—and would, apparently, keep it unnaturally alive for all eternity.

*My God,* I thought.

And then I wondered: was I still a child of God. Or was I rendered into something evil?

I didn't feel evil.

The street was quiet, but not empty. Across the street, the door to my husband's building opened. Two figures emerged. One of them was my husband and the other was a woman. I didn't recognize the woman. He had mentioned acquiring a new secretary a few months back. I hadn't met her. This girl was tall and angular, with straight, blond hair. She wore a very tight white skirt.

They walked together into the adjoining parking lot. He led her to a little red convertible with its top down. At her door my husband put his arms around her waist and gave her a very long, and very deep kiss. They held that position for well over a half a minute. Then she disentangled herself from him, got in the car and drove away. He watched her leave, then turned toward me, and I held my breath. For one brief second I thought he might have been looking at me. Then he turned away, reached for his keys in his pocket, got into his Escalade and left. To drive home to his wife and kids.

Numb, I stayed where I was, the engine off. I was surprised to discover that my hand had unconsciously reached inside my jacket for a gun that wasn't there.

# 40.

Danny and I were lying in bed together.

He was under the covers and I was on top of them. As usual. He was naked and I was completely clothed. As usual. Heat from his recently-showered body emanated from his skin. He had removed the scent of her. What a guy. In the dark, I could see his pale shoulders clearly. I could also see that he was looking away from me, eyes open and staring up.

I rolled from my side onto my back, staring up at the ceiling along with him. The ceiling crackled and swirled with the secret particles of light that only I could see.

"I saw you with her tonight," I said.

"I know."

"You haven't kissed me like that in a long time."

He said nothing. The particles of light seemed to react to the tension around us, swirling faster, agitated.

I said, "You knew I was there and you kissed her in front of me anyway?"

"I saw you immediately when we stepped outside."

"So you gave her a particularly long kiss."

"Yes."

"Why even bother coming home?"

"My kids are here."

My voice started shaking, and I could not hide the fear and the hate. I wanted to rise up and pound his goddamn chest, make him hurt as much as he was hurting me.

"Do you love her?"

"I think so. Yes."

"Do you love me?"

"I don't know. I used to." He paused. "I do not think I can love what you have become. I've tried. I honestly tried. But...."

"I repulse you."

"Yes," he said. "You sicken me and scare the hell out of me, and when I touch you it's all I can do to not gag."

"Words every wife wants to hear."

"I'm sorry, Sam. I really am. I'm sorry that you were attacked. I'm sorry it has come to this. But a marriage is between a man and a woman."

"I am not a woman?"

"I don't know what the hell you are. A fucking vampire, I suppose. And what is that?"

"I'm still the same person."

"No, you're not. You drink blood in the garage like a ghoul. I have nightmares about you. I dream that you attack me in the middle of the night, that you attack our children—that you just lose it and slaughter us all."

I was crying now. Sobbing and crying and completely out of control. This was my worse fear, and it had come to pass. The love of my life was leaving me, and I didn't blame him for one second.

He ignored my crying. In fact, he turned his back to me.

And then I lost it. Just lost it.

In a blink of an eye I was on top of him. Both hands snaked down around his throat, faster than any cobra, faster than he could defend himself. I pinned him to the bed. "You fucking take my kids and I will kill you, you son-of-a bitch. Do you understand? I will hunt you down and kill you and tear you into fucking shreds."

My voice was hysterical, shrieking, piercing. I saw my hands around his muscular neck—my narrow, pale, strong hands. His own were struggling with mine, trying desperately to pry me loose, but no luck. I didn't know if he was getting any air, and I suddenly didn't care. He kicked and convulsed, and still I strangled him, still I cursed and screamed at him. Now my arms shook with the effort. One more second, more pound of pressure per square inch, and I would have killed him, and I would have enjoyed it. At least, in that moment.

Then I released my hold and he rolled off the bed, falling, coughing and gagging and spitting up. His body wrenched with the effort to breathe.

My heart was racing. "Don't you ever take my kids away, Danny," I whispered. "Ever."

# 41.

Danny was sitting up against the headboard, his knees drawn up against his chest. A sort of guy version of the fetal position. He was watching me with wary eyes. Who would blame him?

Although the room was dark, I could see the red welts around his neck. He had regained his breath and I had calmed considerably. The fury that overcame me had nothing to do with the vampire in me, and everything to do with the mother in me.

"I have given strict instruction to my attorney to release sealed information concerning your...*disease*," he said. His voice was ragged and torn, as if he were speaking through a very old microphone. Or a very damaged throat. "That is, should anything suspicious happen to me."

"What do you mean?" I was sitting on the edge of the bed. A sick realization came over me. Danny, despite my threats of bodily harm, would have the upper hand in this situation.

"I've completely detailed everything about your vampirism. Everything. From your attack six years ago to our running account with the butchery in Norco."

"No one will believe it. They'll think you're crazy."

"Maybe, maybe not."

"What does that mean, Danny?"

"I've included in the packet two things. A video of me holding a mirror up to you while you slept, and a vial of your own tainted blood."

"Are you insane?" I asked.

"Maybe. But I want the kids, and I want them safe, and I want you to stay away and keep your filthy hands off me—and them."

We were silent again as I absorbed all of this. I was stuck. Whether or not anyone believed his story or bothered to test the vial of blood was debatable, but one I could not chance. I had known early on that I could never, ever risk being exposed.

"What about the kids?" I asked.

He took a deep breath and drew his knees up higher. "I'm taking the kids, Samantha."

I needed a clear mind for this. He was leaving, that much I understood, that much I could try to deal with. But to take the kids....

When I spoke again, I was the voice of reason and calm. "Danny, baby, listen to me. We've lived like this for six years. I've given them nothing but love. I would never harm anyone, not a living soul, especially not my kids. They need their mother."

He snorted. "After what just happened? My God, Sam, I thought you were going to kill me."

"I was furious, Danny. You've been cheating on me. Hell, you practically flaunted it in my face. Anyone woman —any mother—would have reacted the same way." I paused. He rubbed his neck and winced. "They need their mother, Danny."

"I agree, which is why I will allow you to see them every other weekend. Supervised." He inhaled deeply, raggedly.

He knew what he was doing to me, he knew he was killing me, but he continued on. "Don't fight me on this either, Sam. Don't make me expose you for the monster that you are, because I will. I will do it to save the kids."

"Danny, please."

"I'm sorry. I truly am. You never deserved this to happen to you, and you never asked for it. Neither did I. Neither did the kids. But I am determined to keep them safe. I stuck it out this long, Sam. I did it for the kids. I think they're both old enough now to understand that mommy and daddy's relationship isn't so good anymore."

In a flash of rare compassion, he reached out and took my hand. I noticed he didn't recoil in horror, or hold it limply. He held it firmly and compassionately. "This is for the best, Sam. Now you can live...your life, however you need to life it. You don't have to worry about picking the kids up from school anymore, or about going to parent/teacher conferences, or about staying up with the kids during the day if one is sick. You can be free to be who you are, to be *what* you are, whatever that is...."

He kept talking, but I wasn't sure if I was listening. I could only think of my children growing up without their mother. I could only think of not seeing their faces everyday. Worse, I realized there was nothing I could do short of kidnapping them, and I would never do that because what kind of life would that be? Danny continued talking, extolling the virtues of being on my own, unhindered by the kids and the daily grind of being a mother; he continued stroking my hand, and I knew that my kids were lost to me. Every other weekend seemed an eternity. Suddenly, the daily grind of being a mother never looked better, and every time I tried to state my case the words failed me, because, in my heart, I knew he was right.

*I am a monster. I am unnatural. They deserve better.*
*Bullshit. I'm their mother.*
*No matter what.*

I had always known this day was coming. I had fought against it so hard. I had tried to do everything right and it still wasn't enough.

"If I promise not to fight you, if I promise to give you the kids to raise with whomever you choose, can I ask you one favor?"

He said nothing. Lying next to me, I could almost see him biting his lower lip, as he always did when in deep thought. This hesitation coming from a man who once proposed to me in a hot air balloon even though he had been terrified of heights.

"Please, Danny, just one favor."

"Maybe."

"That I see them every weekend, unsupervised."

He thought about it long and hard. He let out a long stream of breath. "Okay, Sam, every weekend. But I'm afraid I must insist the meeting be supervised."

"Thank you, Danny," I said quietly, my voice full of emotion and pain, unrecognizable even to my own ears. "When will the three of you be leaving?"

And the moment I uttered those words, I realized my mistake. They weren't going anywhere.

"*We* are not leaving, Sam. *You* are leaving, and I want you out by tomorrow night."

# 42.

In the late evening, I was standing on the ninth floor balcony of the Embassy Suites Hotel in Brea.

It had been a rough day. My sister had come over to help me move, although there wasn't really much to move. Mostly she was there for moral support. Danny was there, too, but he wasn't there for moral support. Instead, he watched over me like a prison warden.

Since it was my last day with the children, I had let them stay home from school. Earlier, I tried explaining to them why mommy was going away. I told them it wasn't their fault, that mommy and daddy could not live together anymore, that mommy and daddy still loved each other but not in that special way. They both cried. So did I.

At the hotel, Mary Lou helped me unpack, even the packets of chilled blood, which we stored in the suite's mini-refrigerator. I caught her studying one of the packets. Her face, I noted, had turned white. To her credit, she didn't say anything about the blood, and I silently thanked her for that.

We sat together on my bed and she rubbed my neck and shoulders and gently stroked my hair. Her touch, her warmth, her compassion gave me strength. She didn't think I should be alone and wanted to stay the night with me. I thanked her and told her I wanted to be alone. She didn't like it, but relented, and when she was gone I found myself alone—really alone—for the first time in years.

The suite had a small balcony with two canvas folding chairs and a circular table. I opened the sliding glass door and stepped out onto the balcony, and was immediately blasted by cold wind. The city was so breath-takingly beautiful from up here. Twinkling lights spread in all directions, as far as the eye could see.

In one swift motion, I pulled myself up onto the balcony's wall and hung my feet hung over the ledge. I kicked my feet absently like a kid hanging from a swing.

Cars sped by on the little street that separated the hotel from the nearby mall. Its various parking lots were jammed with cars. Malls and Orange County sort of went hand-in-hand.

I was hungry and, at the same time, sick to my stomach. Sometimes those two went hand-in-hand, as well.

Wind pulled and tugged at me, moaning softly over my ears. It was just after 8:00 p.m. It had been a hell of a shitty day, and I hadn't slept a wink.

The attack six years ago had cost me so much. It had cost me my job, my sunny days, my home, my husband, my kids and my life.

I watched people entering and leaving the big mall, eager to spend their hard earned money at over-priced stores. Even from nine stories up, I could make out details of clothing and facial expressions. Most appeared to be in relatively good moods. Just living the American dream. Nothing better than spending an evening at the mall with the family. Shopping for nice things in nice stores with nice-looking kids. One person, returning a JCPenny bag, didn't look so happy.

Like a hawk watching field mice, I watched it all from above, sitting on the ledge, feeling increasingly separated from the human race.

I stood suddenly, pulling my feet up, balancing easily on the wide ledge.  The wind seemed to pick up, but not enough to threaten to knock me off.

I looked down at the narrow street below, at the bustling mall, the streaming cars, the distant city lights.  Sounds and smells came at me, too.  The occasional, echoing honk of a car horn in an enclosed parking garage.  The murmur of voices. The murmur of children's voices.

I took a deep, worthless, shuddering breath.

I had nothing to lose, really.  My kids had been torn from my life. Hell, my *life* had been torn from my life.

The ground was far, far below.  Nine stories up looks like a hundred and fifty stories up, especially if you are thinking of jumping. And I was thinking of jumping.

I closed my eyes, then leaped off the balcony.

# 43.

Time seemed to slow.

I arched up and out into the night and stretched my arms to either side. I lifted my face to the stars and felt the wind in my hair and experienced a profound and uncommon silence, as if all noise in the world had suddenly been muted. Slowly, I tilted down into a natural dive.

And then I plummeted.

Only then was I aware that perhaps I should have ditched the clothing. I didn't want to be a bat trapped in a cardigan sweater.

By all rights I should die in the next few moments. No one should be able to survive such a fall, perhaps not even a vampire.

A flash of yellow light erupted in my head. And within that light was an image of something black. Something with wings. Something large and alien and frightening.

And then the image disappeared.

The world began to accelerate. The floors to the hotel swept past me. Some of the curtained windows were open. One man dressed only in his tighty-whitties turned suddenly, as if he had seen something in his peripheral vision. He had —a falling woman. But I had swept past him before he could complete his full turn.

Moon Dance

The image of the winged creature reappeared, but this time taking on greater detail. It was vaguely humanoid with great leathery wings. I felt an immediate and powerful affinity for the creature.

A sliver of sidewalk, once only a silver thread from high above, now rapidly grew into a very real sidewalk. A very real *cement* sidewalk. Picking up speed, I past a few more floors. Unfortunately for me, the hotel was running out of floors.

I spasmed suddenly.

The ground rose rapidly to greet me.

I had only seconds.

My clothing burst from my body. A huge set of thickly-membraned wings flapped from my arms and legs like a failed parachute.

The ground was upon me.

I changed position, altered my body.

The flapping skin, stretching from my wrists to somewhere around my mid-thigh, caught the wind and snapped taut. My arms shuddered and I held them firm and veered over the sidewalk with just a few feet to spare. I swept up, instinctively knowing just what I had to do.

My right hip slammed into a No Parking sign.

I lost control, tumbled through the air. And as if some ancient memory of flight had been re-born within me, I somehow regained control and righted myself, and flew low and fast over the mall parking lot, skimming over the roofs of a few dozen gleaming SUVs. I lifted my head and gained some altitude, and very quickly I was above the mall.

I was flying.

*Flying.*

# Moon Dance

Born from an innate knowledge I didn't comprehend or question, I skillfully flapped my wings and propelled myself up into the night sky.

# 44.

I was dreaming, of course.

I had to be. I mean, this really couldn't be happening to me, right?

Any minute now I was going to wake up and discover that I wasn't flying five hundred feet above the city of Brea. That I was back in my hotel room, alone, and miserable.

Dream or no dream, I might as well enjoy the ride.

A blast of wind hit me. I lost control and fumbled through the air. I panicked, until my on-board navigational system kicked in again and I adjusted my wings and lowered my shoulder and smoothed out the ride.

As I flew, and as my panicked breathing returned to normal, I looked over to my right arm. Make that *wing*. The arm appendage was thin and black and deeply corrugated with hard muscle. A thick membrane of leathery skin was attached to my wrist and ran down below my waist.

Below was Randolph Street. I followed it for a few minutes before lowering my right arm, raising my left, and making an arcing turn to starboard. The ability to turn came naturally to me, as if I had been doing this all my life.

Brea was bustling at this hour; it was still early evening, the streets crowded with vehicles. I flew over a section called Downtown Brea, alive with hundreds of people, all moving purposefully from one shop to another. The sky was cloudless, just a smattering of stars. Against this backdrop, my black skin would have been almost invisible to the human eye. Surprisingly, southern California was ideal vampire country.

I decided to experiment.

But first I wanted to see what the hell I looked like. I found a suitable office structure made entirely of glass. I swept past the second floor in hopes of seeing my reflection —and was dismayed to see nothing at all. Same old story.

I swept back up into the sky, flapping hard, gaining elevation. The motion was already fluid and effortless for me. I continued climbing and suddenly wondered how high I dared to go. Already I was many hundreds of feet above the city.

So I continued up, climbing higher and higher.

The sky darkened. The city lights diminished. The wind and cold increased. I felt I could continue forever, tirelessly, across time and space, to other worlds, other stars, other universes. I felt free and alive and for a first time in a long, long time, I did not curse my fate.

I finally stopped ascending and hovered, stretching my arms out, soaring on the currents of space. Orange County shimmered far below. Far off I could see LA and Long Beach. To the south the great black expanse of the Pacific Ocean.

The wind was powerful and relentless. I rocked and absorbed the punishment, battered about like a demon kite. A demon kite with no strings. In this form I knew I could travel the earth. Travel anywhere and everywhere.

I had lost my kids on this day—but gained unlimited freedom. In more ways than one.

# Moon Dance

I tucked in my wings, the membranes collapsing in upon themselves like twin Geisha fans. I rocketed down like a blood-sucking meteorite. The city lights rapidly approached. Adrenalin rushed through my blood stream. I found myself screaming with delight; or, rather, *screeching* with delight. Wind pummeled me. I shook and vibrated and kept my eyes barely above a squint. Natural folds along my cheekbones and brow ridges did wonders to keep my vision clear.

Downtown Brea came back into view, seemingly rising up to meet me. The details of the busy street came rapidly into view, and only at the last possible second did I pull up, lifting my head and opening my arms. The sheer gravitational force on me should have been enough to rip my leathery wings from my arms, but they didn't rip. Instead, performed wonderfully and I swept down the middle of the crowded street, barely above the roofs of the many SUVs and minivans.

People saw me. Many people. They pointed and turned and spilled their drinks and ice creams. But I was already gone, turning hard to port and disappearing down a side street.

The side street led back to the hotel, where I carefully settled on my balcony. At least, what I hoped was my balcony. I was breathing hard. Apparently, I did need oxygen.

My arms were still long, slender and black. The flying membranes, attached to each side of my body, hung behind me like twin capes. As I stood there on my balcony, wondering what the hell I was supposed to do next, a vague image of me as a human appeared in my mind.

I opened my eyes and looked at my arms. They were aglow with pink flesh. I looked down and was not surprised to see that I was entirely naked.

I was back.

# 45.

*I flew tonight.*

I was typing on my laptop, one of the few possessions, outside of clothing and makeup, that I had brought with me. The hotel provided wireless connections, which was one of the reasons I had picked it. That, and because it had nine floors. Somewhere, in the back of my mind, I was planning on making my leap, and the taller the hotel the better.

*You did!?* came Fang's immediate response.

*Yes!*

*You figured this out on your own?*

*Yes.*

*But how?*

I told him the sequence of events leading up to my decision to leap from my balcony. Or, rather, my *impulse* to leap from the balcony.

*I am sorry about your marriage, Moon Dance. Maybe someday you can marry me. I promise to be accepting.*

*I'm not in the mood for jokes, Fang.*

*No joke.*

*Then I'm not in the mood to be propositioned.*

*Sorry.* He paused, then typed: *What was it like, flying?*

*Heavenly. Rapturous. Nothing like it in the world. I will definitely be doing that again.*

*What exactly did you turn into?*

*Something scary. Something nightmarish.*

*But you were still you, right? You could think, feel?*

*Yes, I never left. It was still me, just in the skin of something horrific.*

*Describe it.*

I did, as best as I could. I told Fang that there was really very little of me I could see, other than the image I had in my mind. The image was scary enough.

*What am I?* I asked him when I was through.

*You are a vampire, Moon Dance.*

*But am I even one of God's creatures? Am I something evil? Am I even truly alive?*

*Do you feel alive?*

*Yes.*

*Do you feel evil?*

I thought about that. *I feel like such an aberration, a mistake. Something forgotten. Something to be ignored. Something to fear.*

*Moon Dance?*

*Yes?*

*We all feel that way. You are just different.* He paused. *Do you believe in a Creator?*

I paused, then wrote: *I don't know. I believe in something.*

*Well, do you think that Something has suddenly decided to ignore you because you were attacked and changed into something different against your own free will?*

*I don't know, Fang.*

There was a long pause. *I don't. I don't think a god of creation has suddenly decided to ignore you, Moon Dance. I think, in fact, you have been granted a rare opportunity to do things some people have never thought possible, to express yourself in ways that many people will never, ever experience. You could choose to see this as an opportunity or as a curse. Do you choose to see the good or the bad?*

*So there is good in me?*

*More good than most.*

*So I have not been forgotten?*

*Who could forget you, Moon Dance?*

*Thank you, Fang. Thank you for always being here for* me.

*Always. And Moon Dance?*

*Yes?*

*Take care of yourself. There's people out there who love you.* A long pause. I waited. *And I am one of them.*

*Thank you, Fang, that means a lot. Goodnight.*

*Goodnight, Moon Dance.*

# 46.

On a Thursday night just a little past 9:30 p.m., Detective Sherbet picked me up outside the Embassy Suites. A light rain had been falling and I hadn't bothered with an umbrella.

"Trash night," he said when I slid in next to him. Sherbet was driving a big Ford truck with tinted windows. "Hey, you're all wet."

"I enjoy the rain."

"So enjoy the rain with an umbrella. You're getting my leather seats all wet."

"Get over it. It's just a truck."

"It's not just a truck. It's my baby."

"There's more to life than trucks."

"Someone in a bad mood?" he asked.

"Yes."

He grinned and pulled out into traffic. The truck had a throaty roar. The detective, I quickly discovered, drove like a mad man. He pulled into traffic with reckless abandon, confident that his truck could survive any impact. I found his driving exciting. Maybe I was a closet adrenalin junkie.

"So do you have termites or something?" he asked after a cacophony of horns had subsided behind us.

"Excuse me?"

"Is that why I'm picking you up at a hotel in Brea? Does your house have termites?"

"Oh," I said. "Sure."

"Speaking of Brea, did you hear about the flying creature last night?"

"No."

"Police call centers got swamped last night. About a hundred total. Apparently something dropped out of the sky and swooped down the middle of Downtown Brea."

"Maybe it was a bird," I said distractedly. I didn't feel like talking. I was missing my children, and could not fight the horrible feeling that they were forever lost to me.

"This was no bird." He chuckled and made a right onto State College Blvd. A minute later we were waiting at a stoplight to turn left onto Imperial. Through the side window I noticed a few teenage boys gawking at the truck.

"The boys love your truck," I said.

"They should. It's bitchen."

I laughed, despite myself.

Sherbet continued, "Witnesses say it was black and massive and flying almighty fast."

"What happened to it?"

"Made a right onto Brea Blvd and was gone."

"Did it at least use its turn signal?"

The light turned green. He gunned the truck as if he were in a drag race. He looked over at me and smiled. "You don't seem to believe any of this."

"No," I said. "Do you?"

"Hard to say. A hundred witnesses is a lot of witnesses."

"Mass hallucination?" I suggested.

"Maybe," he said. Or maybe they really saw something."

Sherbet pulled behind a long line of cars waiting for the freeway on-ramp. I had the distinct—and exciting—feeling that Sherbet would have preferred to go *over* the cars.

"You hungry?" he asked suddenly.

"No."

"You sure? You look like you could eat."

"I'm sure."

He pulled out of the line of cars, hung a suicidal turn back onto Imperial Blvd, and headed into a nearby Wendy's drive-thru.

"That was frightening," I said.

"Then why are you smiling?" he asked.

"I guess I like frightening," I said.

He ordered his food and pulled up in line. He said, "The wife tonight made a German dish called *machanka*. She thinks I like it. I haven't had the heart to tell her that I quit liking it fifteen years ago."

"You must love her."

"With all my heart," he said.

"Lucky her," I said.

"Lucky *me*."

He got his food. Two bacon burgers, an order of fries, and a king-sized Coke.

"That'll kill you," I said.

"True," he said. "But on the flip side: no more *machanka*."

Shoving fries into his mouth, he recklessly made a left into traffic, into a break of traffic that was virtually non-existant. He looked at me and grinned around the fries.

I grinned, too.

Soon, we were heading south on the 57 freeway.

# 47.

It was after 10:00 p.m. when we parked on a street that ran perpendicular with Horton's massive Gothic revival.

A thin sheet of rain obscured the street. We sat in the cab of his truck with the engine and wipers off. Moving wipers attracted attention, as did an idling car. So we at in the cold and wet. The house before us was massive and brooding. Its towering gables spiked the night sky. Hawthorne would have been pleased. The truck's tinted glass made the world darker than it really was. I liked darker.

After a moment, Sherbet shook his head. "Who could live in something like that?" Sherbet shuddered. "Like something in a fucking Dracula movie."

"I like it," I said.

"Why does that not surprise me?"

"What does that mean?" I asked.

"Nothing. Just being a wise guy."

Sherbet was still sipping on his king-sized Coke. Occasionally some of the sips turned into loud slurps. The remnants of his greasy meal were wadded into a greasy ball and shoved into the greasy bag. The strong smell of burgers and fries suffused the interior of the truck cab. My hungry stomach was doing somersaults.

*Easy, girl.*

"That your stomach growling?" he asked.

"I don't know. Haven't noticed."

He shook his head and slurped his Coke. The street was mostly empty. Occasionally a big car would splash past, and since tomorrow was trash day, most of the residents already had their trash cans out by the curb. Rick Horton's trash cans were nowhere to be found.

"Maybe he forgot tomorrow was trash day," said Sherbet.

"Maybe."

"Maybe he's one of those procrastinators who runs out just as the trash truck pulls up, dragging their trashcans behind them, beseeching the truck drivers wait."

"Beseeching?" I said.

"It's a word."

"Just not a word you often hear from a cop with a dollop of ketchup on his chin."

He hastily swiped at the dollop, but missed some of it. He licked his finger. "You have good eyes," he said.

"And you have a bad aim." I used one of the napkins to clean his chin.

The rain picked up a little. The drops were now big enough to splatter. Overhead, the weeping willows wept, bent and shuddering under the weight of the rain.

"I could use some coffee," the detective said. "No telling when this guy is coming out with his trash."

So we got some coffee at a nearby Burger King. Or, rather, Sherbet did. He bought me a bottled water.

"You're a cheap date," he commented as he mercifully decided—at the last possible second—that an incoming bus too close to dash in front of.

"And you're the reason fast food establishments stay in business."

"On second thought," he said. "I would never date someone as grouchy as you."

"It's been a bad week."

"Wanna talk about it?"

"No."

He didn't push it. We pulled back up in front of Horton's Gothic revival. Nothing much changed. Horton still hadn't taken out his trash, which was, at least tonight, the object of our interest.

So we waited some more. Investigators are trained to wait. We're supposed to be good at it. Waiting sucks. The interior of the truck was filled with the soothing sound of rain ticking on glass and sheet metal. I sipped some water. Sherbet was holding his coffee with both hands. Steam rose into his face. A light film of sweat collected on his upper lip. The coffee smelled heavenly. Coffee was not on my list. Rivulets of rain cascaded down the windshield. The shining street lamps, as seen through the splattered windshield, were living prisms of light. I watched the hypnotic light show.

"What's it like working for the feds?" Sherbet suddenly asked.

"Safe, secure. Often boring, punctuated with the occasional thrill. My days were endlessly fascinating. I loved my job."

"Do you miss it?"

"Hard to say. I miss the camaraderie of my partners. My job now is a lonely one. When I get the chance to work with someone else I often take it."

"Even with an old dog like me?"

I looked at him. The truck was mostly silent. I heard him breathing calmly through his nose. Could smell his aftershave. He smelled like a guy should smell. Moving shadows from the rain dribbling down the windshield reached his face. The man seemed to like me, but he was suspicious of me. Or perhaps just curious. As a homicide investigator, he had his own highly-attuned intuition, which worried me because I was obviously causing it to jangle off the hook. But I had committed no crime, other than draining a corpse of blood, which I didn't think was a crime, although I'd never perused the penal code for such an article.

"Sure," I said. "Even an old dog like you."

"How reassuring."

Through Horton's wrought iron fence I saw a figure struggling with something bulky. The fence swung open and Horton appeared in a yellow slicker, struggling to wheel a single green trash can. The can appeared awkward to maneuver. Or perhaps Horton was just clumsy. As he deposited the can near the curb, his foot slipped out from under him, sending him straight to his back. I voted for clumsy.

Sherbet shook his head. "Smooth," he said.

# 48.

"Let's wait a few minutes," said Sherbet after Horton had dashed inside. Horton ran like a girl.

"Doesn't look like much of a killer," I said.

"No," said Sherbet. "They never do."

The rain came down harder, pummeling the truck, scourging what appeared to be a custom paint job. Sherbet seemed to wince with each drop.

"Aren't you a little too old to be into cars?" I asked.

"You can never be too old."

"I think you're too old."

"Yeah, well how old are you?"

"I'd rather not say. Not to mention you've looked at my police record and already know."

"Thirty-seven, if I recall," he said. "A very young thirty-seven. Hell, you don't even have a wrinkle."

"I'm sure it will catch up to me someday," I said, and then thought: or not. But I played along. "And before I know it, I'll look into the mirror one day and find a road atlas staring back at me."

He snorted. "Welcome to my world."

We waited some more. The rain continued to pound. Some of the water collected and sluiced along the windshield in shimmering silver streaks. Sherbet and I were warm and secure in our own little microcosm of leather, plastic, wood, and empty Wendy's bags. Here in this mini-world, I was the vampire queen, and Sherbet was my noble knight. Or perhaps my blood slave, from whom I fed.

"Your name always reminds me of ice cream," I said. "I like your name."

"I hate it."

"Why?"

"Reminds me of ice cream."

A light in Horton's upstairs window turned off. The house was dark and silent. So was the street.

"You stay here while I procure the target's trash," Sherbet said. "We're going to have to adhere to some protocol if we hope to get a search warrant out of this."

"Lot of fancy words to basically say you'll be the one getting wet."

"Oh, shut up," he said.

I grinned. "Procure away, kind sir."

"Okay," he said, pulling on his hood. "Here goes."

He threw open his door and dashed off through the rain. His nylon jacket was drenched within seconds. He moved surprisingly well for an older guy. He reached Horton's trash can, pulled open the lid, and removed two very full plastic bags. I was suddenly very much not looking forward to digging through those. He shut the lid, grabbed a bag in each hand, and hustled back to the truck. He deposited both in the bed of his truck.

"You're dripping on the leather," I said when he slid into the driver's seat.

"I know," he said, starting the truck. "It saddens the heart."

# 49.

We drove until we found an empty parking garage adjacent to an ophthalmologist college. The lights inside the garage were on full force and a white security pick-up truck was parked just inside the entrance.

We pulled up beside the truck. The guard was out cold, wrapped in his jacket, hugging himself for warmth, the windows cracked for air. Sherbet rolled down his window. The sound of thumping rain was louder and more intense with the window down. The guard still hadn't moved.

"Hey," said Sherbet.

The man bolted upright, accidentally slamming his hand against the steering wheel. The horn went off and he jumped again, now hitting his head on the cab's ceiling.

Sherbet turned to me. "Night of Ten Thousand Fools."

"An Arabian farce."

The detective leaned out the window, producing his badge from his jacket pocket. "Detective Sherbet, Fullerton PD. We need to, um, commandeer your garage for a few minutes."

"Of course, detective." The guard's voice was slightly high-pitched. He was fortyish and much too small to be taken seriously as a guard. His neck was also freakishly long. "It's the rain, you know. Knocks me out every time.

My bosses found out I was sleeping again, they'd fire me."
He looked sheepish.

"Don't worry about it, pal," said Sherbet. "I won't tell if
you don't."

He brightened, his job secure. "Is there maybe something
I can do for you? You know, maybe help you out?"

"Sure," said Sherbet. "Guard this entrance with your life.
No one comes in."

"You got it, detective!"

Sherbet rolled up his window and we eased into the
parking structure and out of the rain.

"Commandeer the garage?" I said.

"Sounds important."

I looked back. The guard had positioned his truck before
the garage's entrance. "Good of you to give him something
to do," I said. "But what happens if someone wants to come
in?"

"Then they'll have to deal with Flamingo Neck."

I snorted. "Flamingo Neck? Thought he looked more
like a stork."

"Whatever." Sherbet pulled into a slot. "You ready to dig
in?"

"As ready as ever."

The covered garage was mostly empty, save for a few
desolate vehicles. These vehicles had the look of semi-
permanence. Sherbet handed me a pair of latex gloves.

The bags were sodden. One of them stank of rotten
dairy. I gave that one to the detective.

"Thanks," he said.

"I'm a lady," I said. "Ladies don't dig through smelly
trash."

"They do when they're on my shift."

"Yeah, well, luckily I don't work for you."

"Luckily."

With legs crossed, I hunkered down on a parking rebar. I untied the my bag and was immediately greeted with what must have been last night's chicken teriyaki. My stomach growled noisily. My stomach seemed to have missed the memo about my new diet. My new *blood* diet.

*No chicken teriyaki for you, my friend. Ever.*

I removed the big stuff first. An empty gallon of milk that, because it was sealed, had bloated to half again its normal size. Boxes of cereal, an empty jar of peanut butter, many cardboard cases of beer. Someone liked beer. A smattering of plastic Coca-Cola bottles. I sorted through it all, leaving a careful pile to my left.

At the bottom nook was a batch of papers which proved to be torn mail, the majority of which were credit card applications. Smart man. Debt, bad.

"Nothing over here," I said.

I looked over at the detective who was squatting down on one knee. His hands were smeared with gelatinous muck. He looked a little green, and for a homicide detective, that's saying a lot.

"More of the same," he said. "Nothing."

Beyond, the security guard was pacing in the rain before his truck. Occasionally he stole glances at us.

"Same time next week?" Sherbet asked.

"Yes," I said. "More fun."

"And Mrs. Moon?" he said, looking down at his rancid ichor-covered latex gloves. "Next time *you* get the smelly bag."

# 50.

Sherbet dropped me off at the hotel and suggested that I take a shower because I smelled like trash. I told him thanks. At the hotel lobby, the doorman greeted me with a small bow. I could get used to that. Then he crinkled his nose. Maybe I did need to take a shower.

Conscious of my stench, I took the elevator to the ninth floor and inserted my keycard into the lock and pushed the door open and my warning bells went off instantly.

*Someone was inside.*

Movement down the hall. I turned my body, narrowing it as a target, just as an arrow bolt struck me in the shoulder, slamming me hard into the open door, which in turn slammed shut. I ducked and peered through the darkness and there, standing near my open balcony, was a man. A good-looking man. Tall and slender. Silhouetted in shadows. But I could see into shadows. His spiky blond hair looked like a frayed like a tennis ball. He was staring at me down the length of a cocked crossbow.

I knew him. It was the UPS man.

He didn't say anything, didn't move. Simply stood there with his crossbow trained, sweat gleaming on his forehead. His hands were unwavering. A flask of clear liquid was at his hip. There was a cross around his neck and a strand of garlic. He adjusted his sights imperceptibly, and I realized he was searching for a clear shot at my heart. I was determined not to give him that clear shot. I looked at him from over my shoulder.

"Who are you?" I asked.

"You don't need to know."

"Then why are you doing this?" My breath came in short gasps. I needed to do something about the shaft in my shoulder, but I didn't dare take my eyes off the man. The strand of garlic was bullcrap. Hell, I cooked with garlic all the time. But the water on his hip—holy water, no doubt—was troubling. I hadn't dared experiment with holy water.

"It's nothing personal," he said.

"The bolt in my shoulder makes it personal."

"It was meant for your heart."

Behind me I heard voices. Someone was getting off the elevator. The voices were mixed with drunken laughter.

Although I hadn't taken my eyes off the hunter, I had unwittingly shifted my weight to the sound of the voices. Apparently I had exposed my heart. He saw the opening he was looking for, and fired.

I heard the *twang* and *snap* of the bolt leaping from the crossbow. I saw it coming, too. Clearly. Rotating slightly in the air. My world slowed down. Much as it had when I leaped off the balcony.

As it rotated, its metal tip gleaming off of light unseen, my hand was coming up. And just before it buried itself into my heart, I caught the damn thing in the air, snagging it just inches from my chest.

The hunter gaped at me in disbelief, then flung himself backward through the open French doors and vaulted the railing. I pushed away from the doorway, stumbled through the suite and out onto the balcony. It was still raining. I peered down over the ledge and saw a man rappelling down the facade of the building. The rope was attached to the roof above. He dropped down into some foundation brush and unhooked himself. He looked up at me briefly and then dashed off. I watched him disappear around the corner of the hotel.

Back in my suite, out of the rain, I gripped the fletched end of the arrow shaft and winced. *Okay, this is going to hurt.* I inhaled deeply and pulled slowly. The pain was unbearable. I gasped and stumbled into the bathroom. The mirror revealed empty clothing, animated clothing, a miracle of special effects. An arrow protruded from the blouse's shoulder area. A thick wash of blood was spreading down from the shoulder. The sight of the bloodied disembodied clothing was surreal.

I closed my eyes, continued pulling. White flashes appeared behind my eyelids. I pulled harder, screaming now. I looked down once and saw that the metal tip was almost out. I also saw that it was bringing with it a lot of meat from my arm.

Tears streamed from my eyes and I heard myself whimpering and still I continued to pull, and finally the bolt came free, followed immediately by a great gout of erupting blood.

It was then that I fainted.

# 51.

Sometime during the night I awoke in the bathroom to find myself in a pool of my own blood. I was cold and not very shocked to see that the wound in my shoulder had healed completely. I stumbled into the bedroom and collapsed into bed.

I slept through the day and awoke at dusk. I felt like hell, groggy, disoriented. I had to remind myself where I was. I bolted upright. Shit! I had forgotten to pick up the kids!

I was just about to hop out of bed until I remembered it wasn't my job to do so anymore. Danny's mother picked them up now. I slumped back into bed, immediately depressed.

My daytime obligations had vanished. Perhaps that was a good thing in away, since I did not operate well during the daylight hours. And, for the first time since the kids had been taken away from me, I felt—which was immediately accompanied by a lot of guilt—a sense of freedom. No kids to pick up. No dinners to cook, no husband to attend to or worry about.

Freedom and guilt, in just that order.

I stretched languidly on the bed, reveling in the surprisingly soft mattress. Why had I not noticed how soft the mattress was? A moment passed, and then another, and then my heart sank.

I had no children to pick up from school and no one to cook for! I missed my kids—but not my husband. Knowing I repulsed him helped sever my emotional ties to him. Yes, I missed the good times with Danny. But I wouldn't miss these past few years.

But I would see my children this weekend. It sucked, but there was nothing I could do about it now, although I vowed to get them back.

Somehow.

For now, though, there was nothing to do but lie here and hurt—and wait for true night to fall. The drapes were thick and heavy and kept out most of the setting sun. My window dressings at home were, in fact, the same heavy curtains found in hotels. Early on, right after my attack, I had wanted to board up the windows, but Danny resisted and we compromised with the heavy drapes.

I massaged my shoulder. Although it still ached, there was no evidence of a wound. Another few inches over and I would have been dead. My only saving grace had been a last-second alarm that went off in my head, a warning that told me to *turn dammit.*

I thought of the vampire hunter. I couldn't have him taking potshots at me whenever he damned well felt like it. I had to do something about him, and short of killing him—which was a definite option—I just wasn't sure just what yet.

First things first. I needed to figure out how the hell he kept showing up without me spotting him. I always check for tails, a good habit for an investigator to have. So I was certain he wasn't following me.

# Moon Dance

Of course, there are other ways to keep tabs on people, especially tabs on vehicles.  In fact, at HUD, we had employed such techniques. Tracking devices.

As I waited for the sun to set, I turned on the boob tube and flipped through some news channels and a re-run or two until I came across an Angels game.  I couldn't recall the last time I watched an Angels game.  I loved baseball, especially the leisurely pace of the game.  I liked the quiet moments when the pitcher stepped off the mound and gathered his thoughts while the world waited.  My father was a minor league pitcher in Rancho Cucamonga.  He was good, but not great, which is why he never made passed single A ball.  Still, surrounded by my ~~five~~ three older brothers, I learned to love the game at an early age.

The Angels were up 3-2.  Tim Salmon had just hit a line-drive single up the middle.

Those childhood memories seemed to belong to someone else.  Someone I barely recalled, yet remembered in detail.  I was a different person now.  The pre-attack Samantha as opposed to the post-attack Samantha were two different people. Hell, two different *species*.

Salmon had a nice butt. So did most baseball players.

I rubbed my shoulder again as I watched the game.  So how the hell did it heal so quickly?  What caused this to happen?  Ancient magic?  If so, was this the same magic keeping me alive?  Was I even truly alive?  Or was I dead and didn't know it?

Bengie Molina, the Angel's catcher, ripped a line drive back to the pitcher.  The pitcher doubled-up Salmon at first.  End of inning.

Perhaps I was nothing more than a spirit or a ghost who didn't have enough sense to move on.  But on to where?  I didn't feel dead.

It was the eighth inning, and the Angels brought in their closer, *El Toro*, the bull. Percival was a big man with big legs. He looked like a bull. I liked the way he squinted and curled his tongue. He looked like a gunslinger. Except this gunslinger slung baseballs. He struck out the first batter in four pitches.

Perhaps I was a plague on the earth, an abnormality that needed to be cleansed. Perhaps the world would have been better off if the vampire hunter's arrow had hit home.

More squinting from El Toro. I heard once that Percival needed to wear glasses but he chose not to while pitching, forcing himself to focus solely and completely on the catcher's signals, blocking out all other distractions. On his next pitch, the batter popped out to center field.

Perhaps I didn't need to know what kept me alive. Perhaps my existence was no more a mystery than life itself. Hell, where did any of us come from? That thought comforted me.

Percival struck out the next batter and pumped his fist. It was the bottom of the eighth inning.

I was suddenly content and at peace with myself. I would have ordered room service if fresh plasma was on the menu. Instead, I sipped from a bottle of water and let the day slip into night. And when the sun finally set, when my breathing seemed unrestricted and my body fully alert, I was ready to take on the world.

Oh, and the Angels won.

With all the time on my hands, maybe I'll catch a night game this season.

# 52.

I first headed over to an auto repair shop in Fullerton.

The young mechanic came out to meet me as I pulled in front of an empty service garage. He wore a light blue workshirt with the name *Rick* stitched on a patch over his chest.

"Sorry, we're closing," said Rick when I rolled down my window.

I pulled out a twenty dollar bill. "All I need for you to do is lift my van."

"Why?"

"I want to have a look underneath."

"*You* want to? Why?"

"Because this is how I spend my Friday nights. Just lift the van for a few minutes, let me have a look underneath, and the twenty is yours."

Rick thought about, then shrugged. "Hey, whatever you say, lady," he said and took the twenty.

He motioned me forward. I drove into the narrow space, straddling the lift. I got out and Rick manipulated some nearby controls and soon the above-ground lift was chugging into action. The van rose slowly, wheels sagging down. A few minutes later, now at eye level, I thought the minivan looked forlorn and sort of helpless, like a wild horse being airlifted from an overflowing river.

"Okay," Rick said. "Have at it. Just don't hurt yourself. You need a flashlight?"

"No,"

"So what are you looking for?" he asked, standing next to me.

"I'll know it when I see it."

The underside of the van was a mess of hoses, encased wires and steel shafts and rods. I walked slowly along the frame until I found it. Held in place by magnets and twisty-ties, the tracking device was about the size and shape of a cell phone.

"What the hell is that?" asked Rick.

"My TV remote," I said. "Been looking everywhere for it."

"No shit?" he said.

"No shit."

# 53.

It took two nights of waiting before I saw the hunter again.

I had left the minivan parked in an alley behind a Vons grocery store. I knew the hunter would eventually investigate, and to do so he would have to physically enter the alley. A typical ambush, and I'm sure he suspected a trap. If so, he would be right. This *was* a trap.

I sat on top of the grocery store roof, near a huge rotating vent. My great, leathery wings were tucked in behind me. The night was warm, but the breeze cooled things down. My skin was thick and rubbery. My new hide did wonders for keeping me warm, especially in the higher altitudes. I had discovered that I could remain in this form for as long as I wished. This was a good discovery, as it was nice shedding my old skin for this new one. People should try it sometime.

The alley was dark and mostly forgotten. My minivan attracted very little interest, even from hooligans. So that's why when the bum appeared I perked up.

In my new form, my eyesight was razor sharp and eagle-like, an obvious necessity to high-flying predators. (And thinking of myself as a *high-flying predator* was almost too weird to, well, think about.) The bum was pushing a shopping cart filled to overflowing with what appeared to be junk. I immediately recognized the handsome face, the rugged jaw, the striking blue eyes, and the spiky blond hair shooting out from under a dirty and warped Dodger cap.

*Nice costume, asshole.*

As an added touch, he even dragged his leg a little behind him. The hunter was putting on quite a show, even hunching his shoulders now Quasimodo-like. I couldn't help but smile. At least, I *think* I smiled. It was hard to tell; plus, I wasn't even sure I had lips. At any rate, I *intended* to smile. Anyway, his shopping cart was, in fact, filled to the brim with soda cans. I wondered if he had purchased the cart and cans from a real bum, or collected the cans himself.

*Probably just stole it*, I thought.

He continued slowly down the alley, his head sweeping from side to side. Unfortunately for him, he never thought to look *up*. About fifty feet from the van, he removed a camouflaged crossbow from inside his tattered jacket. He armed it quickly with a bolt,. And then held it out in front of him like a gun.

He approached my van very, very carefully, leaving behind his cart full of cans. He went slowly from window to window, peering inside with a flashlight. I noted he had forgotten to limp.

I stayed put and waited for my opening.

He tried the doors, discovered they were locked, then popped one open with a Slim Jim. He goofed around inside a bit. Reappearing again, frowning. He seemed a bit perplexed. If anything, I had successfully confused the bastard.

The back door to the grocery store suddenly opened, yellow light splashing out into the alley. A kid appeared, hauling a big blue trash can.  The hunter, distracted, turned toward the kid.

*Now!*

I leaped from my perch above.

# 54.

I tucked in my arms and shot down.

The hunter's back was still to me. Wind thundered in my ears. The ground came up fast. More importantly, the hunter's broad shoulders came up fast.

At the last possible second, I spread my wings wide. The leathery hide snapped open like a parachute. The hunter turned at the sound, swinging his crossbow around, but he was too late. My outstretched talons snatched him up by the shoulders. He cried out, screaming like a school girl. The crossbow tumbled away, skittering over the ground. I beat my wings powerfully, once, twice and finally lifted him off his feet and then slowly up out of the alley. He weighed a lot. More than I was prepared for. My arms and wings were strained to the max.

He struggled, kicking, as his arms were now pinned to his sides. He kicked the air futilely. We rose slowly into the sky together. I looked down in time to see the kid running back into the store. I think he wet himself.

Up we went. I was growing stronger, getting used to the added weight. The air grew colder. The hunter should be warm enough thanks to his homeless costume, which consisted of many layers of clothing.

# Moon Dance

I looked down just as he looked up. His face had drained of all color. He looked terrified. He should be terrified. A creature from his nightmares had snatched him away and for all he knew I was going to drop him into an active volcano. Not that there were many active volcanoes in Southern California.

Orange County spread before us, its hundred of thousands of blinking lights evidence that Thomas Edison had certainly been on to something. We flew over Disneyland, which glittered like its own happy constellation. Perhaps park guests would later report seeing a parade float gone amuck.

We reached the beach cities and finally the black ocean itself. Without the city lights, we were plunged into darkness. He stiffened here, and I think he might have whimpered. No doubt he thought I was going to drop him in. I still hadn't ruled it out.

Much later, perhaps assuming he was safe, the hunter relaxed and sagged into my talons. His spoke to me now, his voice rising up to me along with the smell of sea salt and brine, "How is your shoulder, Samantha Moon?"

The sound of my own name startled me. That this flying creature had a name was hard to believe. I didn't bother answering. Even to my own ears my voice was nothing more than a shriek.

He went on, "I suppose you can't speak in your changeling form. That's fine, I'll do all the talking. I know you've had a hell of a shitty week. I saw your children get taken away from you. And probably the last thing you needed was an arrow in your shoulder. So I guess what I'm trying to say is I'm sorry."

*Apology accepted,* I thought. I was nothing if not forgiving.

I continued at a steady pace, wings flapping smoothly and effortlessly, propelling us over the eternal black ocean. I adjusted endlessly to the varying wind conditions.

"I've never seen a vampire with a family before. You have two beautiful children. At first I thought the family was just a facade. Perhaps you were just courting these mortals for your own nefarious means. A new angle, you know, to acquire blood. So I assumed you were hideous and vile to formulate such a scheme. Until I saw that this was indeed *your* family. The little girl is your spitting image."

He stopped talking, and the silence that followed was filled with the rippling of water over the ocean's surface, and something else, something deep and unfathomable, perhaps the sound of millions upon millions of megatons of water turning and roiling and moving over the face of the earth. The ocean's song, if you will, and it was beautiful and haunting.

The hunter told me about himself. His name was Randolf, and his brother, years ago, had been killed by a vampire. Randolf devoted his life to finding his brother's killer, and in the process to kill every vampire he came across.

*Ambitious,* I thought. *But problematic for me.*

His search eventually led him to an old vampire living in a mansion in Fullerton. Randolf ambushed him, killing him with a bolt through the heart. In going through the old vampire's papers, Randolf had come across my name.

He had, in effect, found the vampire who had attacked *me.*

Not just found him. Found him and killed him. Saved me a lot of trouble.

Randolf continued, "But he was not my brother's killer. I still have some unfinished business." He paused. "You are not like other vampires, Samantha. May I call you Samantha?"

I nodded; I'm not sure he saw me nod.

"In your hotel room I found packets of cow and pig blood in your refrigerator. You are not a killer. Not like the others."

I glanced down. He was still wearing the dirty Dodger cap. His spiky blond hair trailed over his ears. His face was purple with cold.

I continued steadily out to sea. I found that distinguishing the black water from the black sky was difficult, but my innate compass kept us on a clear course, and my equally innate horizontal balance kept us from plunging into the ocean. I thought of the old joke: *I just flew in from Chicago, and boy are my arms tired....*

But my energy seemed limitless, even hauling a full grown man. Still, I didn't want to fly too far out to sea; I needed to provide for enough time to safely return before the sun's ascent.

In the far distance, on the surface of the ocean, I spied the twinkling of lights. I altered course and headed toward the lights. Randolf snorted from below. I suspected he had been dozing. A hell of a rude awakening for him, no doubt, hanging from the claws of a flying beast.

The lights turned out to be a ship. In fact, it was a cruise ship.

"You're taking me to the ship," he said.

*Smart boy.*

"I get the hint," he said, laughing. "You want me to stay away. And thank you for not killing me."

There was a lot of activity on the deck of the cruise ship, so I circled the control tower, and set the hunter on the roof of the cabin. Whether anyone saw a black shape descend from the sky remained to be seen.

Randolf scrambled to his feet, no worse for wear. As I hovered above, as he held down his baseball cap against the downdraft of my wings, his astonishing blue eyes caught the starlight. He really was kind of hunky—even to a creature of the night.

He called up to me, "Have a safe flight home, Samantha Moon. Oh, and any idea where I'm headed?"

I had no idea.

I circled once and headed back home.

# 55.

Kingsley looked far more robust and pink than when I had last seen him.

We were at Mulberry Street Cafe in downtown Fullerton, sitting next to the window. It was raining again and the sidewalk was mostly empty of pedestrians. The rain had a trickle-down effect, if you will. Mulberry's was quieter than normal.

Kingsley was wearing a long black duster, and leather Sole gloves, which he removed upon sitting. His dark slacks were darker where the rain had permeated. His face had a rosy red hue and his hair was perfectly combed. He was clean shaven and smelled of good cologne. He was everything a man should be. Gone were the tufts of hair along the back of his hand.

Pablo the headwaiter knew me well. He looked slyly at Kingsley, perhaps recalling that my husband was usually the man sitting across from me. The waiter was discreet enough not to say anything. He took our drink orders and slipped away.

"I'm impressed," said Kingsley, glancing out the window. "Whenever I come here they seat me in the back of beyond."

"They happen to like me here."

"Pretty girls get all the breaks."

"You think I'm pretty?"

"Yeah," said Kingsley. "I do."

"Even for a vampire?"

"Even for a vampire."

Our drinks came. Chardonnay for me and bourbon and water for the counselor. Kingsley ordered shrimp tortellini and I had the usual. Steak, rare.

"You can eat steak?" he asked.

"No," I said. "But I can suck the blood out of the carcass."

"Should make for an interesting show."

"Yes, well, it's the only way I can participate in the human dining experience."

"Well, you're not missing much, "said Kingsley. "Food nowadays is entirely processed, fattening and just plain horrible for you."

"Does it still taste good?"

"Wonderful."

"Asshole."

He laughed. I drank some of my wine. Kingsley, no doubt due to his massive size, often garnered curious glances from both men and women. I think, perhaps, he was the strongest-looking man I had ever seen.

"Are we human, Kingsley?" I asked suddenly.

He had been raising his glass to his lips. It stopped about halfway. "Yes," he said, then raised it all the way and took a sip. He added, "But are we mortals? No."

"Then what makes us *immortal*? Why don't we die like everyone else? What keeps us alive?"

"I don't know."

"Surely you must have a theory."

He sighed. "Just a working hypothesis."

"Let's have it."

"I think it's safe to say that you and I hover on the brink of the natural and the supernatural. So therefore both natural and unnatural laws apply simultaneously. I believe we are both human...and perhaps something greater."

"Sounds lofty."

"Do you suspect we're something *less*?" he asked.

I thought about that. "No. We are certainly not less."

The waiter came by and dropped off some bread. I didn't touch it, but Kingsley dug in. "You mind?" he asked.

"Knock yourself out," I said. "So what are we, then? Some supernatural evolutionary hybrid?"

He shrugged. "Your guess is as good as mine."

"Maybe we are super humans."

"Maybe."

"But during the day I certainly don't feel super. I feel horrible."

"Because our bodies are still governed by some physical laws, along with...other laws. Mystical laws perhaps, laws unstudied and unknown to modern science." He looked at me and shrugged. "Who put these laws into place is anyone's guess. But they're there nonetheless. For instance, one such law dictates I will turn into a wolf every full moon cycle; another dictates you drink only blood."

Kingsley spread liberal amounts of honey butter over his bread. He seemed particularly ravenous. Maybe it was the animal in him.

"Perhaps we are the result of a powerful curse," I suggested.

"Perhaps."

"That makes sense to me, to some degree."

He shrugged. "I'm not sure anyone really knows."

I suspected someone out there *might* know something. Be it vampire, werewolf or something else, something greater perhaps.

I said, "The curse angle could be why holy water debilitates a vampire."

He shrugged. "Sure."

"So to sum up," I said. "We are both natural and supernatural, abiding by laws known only to our kinds."

"And even much of that is open to speculation. For all I know you are part of one long, drug-induced dream I'm still having in the sixties."

Our food came. Kingsley watched me cut a slice of meat from the raw steak, swirl the slice in the splatter of blood, raise the dripping piece to my lips, and suck it dry.

"Sort of sexy," he said. "In a ghoulish way."

I shook my head, then told him about my adventures with the vampire hunter.

He slapped his knee when I was finished. "A Carnival cruise ship?"

"Yes, headed for Hawaii, I think."

"Then let's hope he stays there."

"Yeah," I said. "Let's hope, although he was kind of cute."

"Oh, God."

I reached down into my purse and pulled out the medallion. It was wrapped in a white handkerchief. I unwrapped it for him.

"What's that?" Kingsley asked.

"It was worn by my attacker six years ago."

"Your attacker?"

"The vampire who rendered me into what I am now."

"How did you get it?"

I told him the vampire hunter, his dead brother, and the UPS package. When I was finished, Kingsley motioned toward the medallion. "Do you mind?"

"Knock yourself out."

He picked it up carefully, turned it over in his hand. The gold and ruby roses reflected brightly even in the muted light.

"So why did he give you this?" asked Kingsley.

"I think he was sort of feeling me out, seeing what he was up against. To him, the medallion had no meaning."

"And to you it does?"

I told Kingsley about my dreams. I left out the part where he ravaged me in the woods.

"Those are just dreams, Samantha," he said, studying the heavy piece, turning it over in his big hands. "I've never seen this before."

"But could you look into it for me?" I asked.

"I'll see what I can do," he said. "Do you mind of I take it?"

"Go ahead."

He pocketed the medallion. We continued eating. Outside, a couple sharing an umbrella stopped and examined the menu in the window. She looked at him and nodded. He shrugged. They stepped inside. Compromising at its best.

"Sometimes I think God has forgotten about me," I said.

"I know the feeling."

"That, in fact, I have somehow stumbled upon the loophole of life."

"Loophole?"

"Like you being a defense attorney," I said. "You look for an ambiguity in the law, an omission of some sort, something that allows you to evade compliance."

He nodded, "And being a creature of the night is the ambiguity of life?"

"Yeah. I'm the omission."

"Well, that's certainly one way of looking at it."

"What's another way?"

"To make the most of the life we're given," he said. "To see life—even for the undead—as a great gift. Imagine the possibilities, Samantha? Imagine the good you can do? Life is precious. Even for those who exists in loopholes."

I nodded, thinking of Fang. "Someone told me something like that recently."

"It's good advice," said Kingsley. "In fact, it's good advice for everyone."

"So we are like everyone?"

"No," he said, reaching across the table and taking my hand. His was so damn warm...mine must have felt like a cold, wet, limp noodle in his own. Self-conscious, I almost pulled my hand away, but he held it even tighter, and that warmed my cold, bitter heart.

He said, "No, Sam. We are *not* like everyone else. I'm a wolf in sheep's clothing, and you're a blood-sucking fiend. Granted, a very *cute*, blood-sucking fiend."

# 56.

On a Wednesday night I broke back into Rick Horton's Gothic revival.

I found the same box under the same bed. The file on me now contained a photograph of my home and a picture of me getting into my van. The picture was taken with a telephoto lens from a great distance away. I studied the picture closely; I so rarely saw myself these days. My face was, of course, blurry, but my body looked strong and hard. A diet of blood will do that to you. The picture was taken during the day, and I could see the sun screen gleaming off my lathered cheeks. My hair was hidden in a wide straw hat. I had probably been on my way to pick up the kids from school.

In another file, the same one I had seen the first time I broke in, I found a computer print-out that chronicled in excruciating detail the day in the life of Hewlett Jackson, Kingsley's now-murdered client. The paper had notes written in the margins. One of the hand-written notes said: "Not at work. No access." Another note said: "Not in front of his children."

*Yeah, this would do nicely.*

I pocketed it and returned the box under the bed. In the backyard, with his ferocious guard dogs cowering in the bushes, I wadded up the note in my gloved hands and carefully stuffed it in an empty cereal box in Horton's trash can.

Tomorrow was trash day.

* * *

The next night, Sherbet and I were in the same parking structure being guarded by the same rent-a-cop. The same two vehicles were in the same two parking slots. The only difference tonight was that there was no rain.

I extracted the wadded up piece of incriminating evidence from the cereal box and made a big show of it.

Sherbet took the crinkled paper from my hand and studied it closely. He then squinted at me sideways, studying *me* closely, suspicious as hell. I innocently showed him the cereal box where I had found the note. Finally, after some internal debate, a slow smile spread over his face.

"I think we've got our man," he said.

"I do, too."

"And you had nothing to do with this note?"

"I have no idea what you're talking about, detective."

"Let's go," he said. And go we did.

# 57.

I was leaving the hotel suite to see my children for the first time in a week when my cell phone rang. It was Sherbet.

"You did good work, Mrs. Moon."

"What do you mean?"

"Based on the evidence in the trash can a judge granted us a search warrant. We went through the house yesterday and today we arrested Rick Horton. We found enough incriminating evidence to convict two men for murder."

"I'm not sure that analogy makes sense."

"It doesn't have to. You know what I mean." He paused. "You are a hell of a detective."

"That's what they tell me."

"So why don't you sound happy?" he asked.

"I am very happy. One less killer walking our streets."

We were silent. Sherbet took in some air. "You don't think we got the right guy, do you?"

"I was hired to find out who shot Kingsley Fulcrum," I said. "Did you get Horton's phone records?"

"Of course."

"Could you fax them to me."

"Why?"

"Just humor me."

There was a long pause. Static crackled over the phone line. Finally, I heard him sigh deeply. "Where do I fax them?"

I gave him the number to the courtesy fax machine at the hotel's business center.

"How many months back do you want?" he asked.

"Four months."

"You don't have to do this," he said. "The case is closed."

"I know," I said. "But this detective never sleeps."

"Well, not at night, at least. And Mrs. Moon?"

"Yes?"

"Someday we're going to discuss the eyewitnesses that claim to have seen a man rappel down from your balcony."

"Sure."

"And we're definitely going to discuss the kid who worked at Vons who reported seeing a winged creature carry off a man."

"Sure."

"I don't have any idea what the fuck is going on, but we will talk again."

"I understand," I said. "And detective?"

"Yes?"

"You might have a better idea than you think."

He paused, then hung up.

# 58.

It was the first time I had been back to my home in over a week.

The house itself sat at the end of a cul-de-sac, with a chain link fence around the front yard. Early on I had hated that ugly chain link fence and wanted it torn down. Danny argued against it stating it might prove useful. He was right. The fence kept my young children away from the street, corralled puppies and kittens, bikes and loose balls, and was perfect for stringing Christmas lights along. It was also used as a sort of giant pegboard. We attached posters, artwork and ribbons to it. Advertised their lemonade stands and the birth of any puppies or kittens. I missed that damn fence.

Last year, Danny made us get rid of our dog and cat. The kids were traumatized for months. I think Danny secretly feared I would kill our family pets and feed from them, although he never admitted his concerns to me.

Anyway, now the fence was bare and there were no children playing in the yard. No balls, and certainly no puppies or kittens. Danny's Escalade was parked dead center of the driveway. Usually he parked to the far left half to give my minivan room on the right. He didn't have to worry about that now.

I parked on the street, headed up to the house. The sun was still out and I felt weak as hell, but that wouldn't stop me.

Danny yanked open the door as soon as I reached the cement porch. He stared down at me gravely. He couldn't have seemed less happy to see me. He was as handsome as ever, but that was lost on me now. I only saw his fear and disgust.

"I only have a few minutes, Samantha. These meeting's are terribly inconvenient for me."

"Then leave," I said.

"I can't do that."

"Why?"

He stepped in front of me. "For the protection of my children, that's why."

I pushed him aside and entered my house. "Where are they?"

"In their room. You have only a few minutes, Sam. The baby sitter will be arriving and I am leaving on my date."

I tried to ignore his hurtful words. Mostly, I tried to keep calm and my voice from shaking. "We had agreed on two hours, Danny."

"Things change, Sam," he said dismissively, and I caught the undercurrent of his words. Things change...and so do humans. Into vampires.

He led the way forward and rapped on the children's door. "Kids," he said stiffly. Danny never had a way with our kids. They were always treated like junior assistants, interns or paralegals. "Your mother is here. Come along."

The bedroom door burst open. Little Anthony, with his mess of black curls, flung himself into my arms. Tammy followed a half second later. Their combined weight nearly toppled me over. Squatting, I held their squirming bodies in my arms. Anthony pulled away and I saw that he was still clutching his Game Boy. Neither hell nor high water would separate him from his Game Boy.

"When are you coming back, mommy?" Anthony asked.

Before I could answer, Danny stepped in. "I told you, son, that your mother is not coming back. That she is sick and she needs to stay away."

I almost dropped the kids in my haste to stand and confront Danny. "Sick? You told them I was sick?"

He pulled me away into a corner of the living room, out of range of the children. "You are sick, Samantha. Very sick. And if I had my way I would report you and have you committed—for your safety and the safety of everyone around you."

"Danny," I said carefully, "I am not sick. I am a person like you. I have a problem that I am dealing with. The problem does not control me. I control it."

"Look, whatever. It's easier for the children to accept that you are sick. I'm going to have to demand that you play along with this, Sam."

I stared at him some more, then headed back to the kids. The three of us sat together on the edge of Tammy's bed while they both chattered in unison. They wanted assurance that I would not die, and I guaranteed them that I would never, ever die. Danny rolled his eyes; I ignored him.

And much too soon, I was back in my minivan driving away, crying.

# 59.

My sister came by my hotel suite, bearing with her a bottle of merlot.

Now we were sitting on my bed, legs tucked under us, sipping from our glasses. Mary Lou was on her second glass and already buzzed. I was nowhere near being buzzed. In fact, my last buzz had been when I sucked the blood out of the gang-banger.

"So your case is over?" said Mary Lou.

"Yes, I suppose."

"You suppose?" she asked. "It was in the paper. The police found their man. Your name wasn't mentioned of course. Although that hunky detective had his mug on the front page. Sherbert or something."

"Sherbet," I corrected. "And he is kind of hunky, huh?"

She shrugged. "In a grizzly bear sort of way."

"Sometimes that's the best way."

"Sometimes," she said. "So why do you *suppose*?"

"I think we got the wrong guy."

"The detective seems to think you got the *right* guy."

"We're missing something, I'm not sure what."

"Tell me about it?," she said, topping off her glass. "Walk me through it, maybe I can help you."

"Perhaps you could have helped before you started on your third glass."

"You know I'm very lucid when I drink. Give me a shot. Lay it on me."

And so I did. Everything, from working through the files with Kingsley's secretary, Sara, to the multiple break-ins and the subsequent arrest.

"Other than the fact I don't agree with you tampering with evidence," said Mary Lou, "I don't see any holes here. Horton had the evidence, the files. He had the motive, and he even had a similar weapon registered to him."

"I have no doubt he killed Kingsley's client," I said.

"You just don't think he was the shooter who attacked your attorney."

"No," I said. "I don't."

"Why?"

"For one, they don't look alike."

"He was wearing a disguise," said Mary Lou, over enunciating her words, as she always did when she drank. "Anyone who's seen the video knows that was a fake mustache."

"Horton was clumsy," I said. "Sherbet and I watched Horton struggle with a trash can, and then slip and fall on his ass. He was as athletic as a warthog."

"I don't understand."

"The killer was athletic. Damn athletic. At one point in the video, he leaps smoothly over a bench—"

"And shoots him," said Mary Lou. "Yeah, I remember that. I re-watched the video after you took this case. That stood out. Wow, you're good, sis."

I shrugged. "Still don't know who he is."

"Maybe it's not a *he*," said Mary Lou.

Something perked up within me. "What do you mean?"

"What about his sister? Didn't you mention Horton had a sister?"

I nodded. "She lives in Washington state and is currently recuperating from a broken ankle she suffered a month ago. She was in no condition to shoot and jump over a bench."

"How do you know this?" she asked.

"I'm not considered a super sleuth for nothing."

"Do you think Horton was working alone?"

"I don't know," I said. My gut told me no, but I didn't say anything.

"You going to drink that?" asked Mary Lou, motioning for my glass. I gave it to her. She poured the contents of mine into what was left of hers. "And, since I know you like the back of my hand, you won't rest easy until you find the shooter."

"No," I said, "I won't."

"Perhaps you won't have to wait long, especially if he has an accomplice."

"What do you mean?"

"You were third on the hit list. Perhaps the accomplice will find you."

"Perhaps," I said. "And for the record, I *never* rest easy."

# 60.

An hour after Mary Lou left the hotel phone rang.

I had been staring down at the lights of Brea, lost in my own thoughts, when the phone rang, startling me. I nearly jumped out of my pale, cold skin at the sound of the ringing phone. I answered it.

"Hello?"

"Mrs. Moon?"

"Yes."

"It's the front desk. We have a fax waiting for you in the lobby."

"Thank you. I'll be down in a minute."

With the fax in hand and back in my hotel room, I hunkered down in one of the straight-back chairs and started reading. The cover letter was printed in tight, unwavering letters. Very cop-like. No surprise since the fax was from Sherbet. In his cover letter, he reminded me that the information contained within was confidential. He also reminded me that the case was closed, that he was looking to retire soon, and the last thing he needed was for me to make his life more difficult. He signed his name with an awkward happy face: the eyes were off-set and the mouth was just a long ghoulish gash, a sort of perversion of the

Wal-Mart happy face. I wondered if this was Sherbet's first happy face. Ever.

The rest of the fax consisted of Rick Horton's phone records spanning the last four months. Riveting reading to be sure, so I settled in with a packet of chilled hemoglobin. I flipped through the records methodically, because I am nothing if not methodical. Anyone with eternity on their side damn well better be methodical. I read each number. I looked at dates and times and locations. Most of it was meaningless, of course, but some information began to emerge. First, Rick Horton was obsessed with his sister. A half dozen calls were made to his sister in Washington state each day. Second, Horton had made a handful of calls to Kingsley's office. In fact, eighteen calls in all. Prank calls? Or had Kingsley been in personal contact with Horton?

Next, I searched for key dates and key times and was not really surprised to discover that an hour or so before both Kingsley's shooting and the Hewlett Jackson murder a telephone call had been placed to the same unknown number. It was a local number.

I dialed the number from my hotel phone, which should be untraceable. I waited, discovered that my heartbeat had increased. I was calling the true killer, I was sure of it. In fact, I felt more than sure. I just *knew*.

The line picked up.

A generic voice mail message. I hung up. Maybe I should have left a nasty little message. Then again, I didn't want to scare the killer away, as ironic as that sounds.

Instead, I flipped open my address book and called my ex-partner, Chad Helling. He didn't answer. Typical. I left Chad a voice mail message asking for a trace on the cell number. Once done, I stepped back to the window, pulled aside the curtain and continued staring down at the city.

Moon Dance

# 61.

An hour later, still at the window, my cell rang.

The name that popped up on the LCD screen said it was Sara Benson, Kingsley's receptionist. "Mr. Kingsley Fulcrum requests a meeting tonight at the Downtown Grill in Fullerton at ten thirty."

"Oh, really?" I said, rolling my eyes. "And why doesn't Mr. Kingsley Fulcrum call me himself?" I emphasized *Kingsley Fulcrum*. I mean, who has their secretary set up dates for them? Not only was I falling for a werewolf, I was falling for a werewolf with a massive ego.

"He's in a meeting at the moment."

I checked my watch. Geez, defense attorney's kept weird hours. *Talk about the pot calling the kettle black.*

"Fine," I said. "Tell Kingsley I'll be there."

"I'm sure he will be pleased."

More than likely this was a business meeting, but since this was Friday night, who knows, maybe Kingsley had something more on his mind.

As I was getting dressed for what might or might not be a date, my cell rang again.

"Funny how you only call when you need something," said the deep voice immediately. It was Chad.

"Would you prefer I called if I didn't need something?"

"Would be a pleasant change."

"I'll think about it."

"How's that skin disease working out for you?" he asked.

"Very well, thanks for asking."

"Anytime," he said. "You want the name and address for that cell number?"

"Would be nice," I said, very aware that the name he was about to give me could very well be the shooter.

He gave me the name and address. I used the hotel stationery and pen. By the time I finished writing, my hand was shaking.

I clicked off and stared at the name.

# 62.

I parked in the half-full parking lot. Ever the optimist.

I was wearing flats, which slapped loudly on the swath of cobblestones that led up to the rear entrance of the restaurant. The night was clear and inviting, and I had a sudden surge of hope, and love of life. I felt that all was right in the world, or would be, and for the first time I actually believed it. Hell, I almost felt sorry for people who were not vampires, who did not get to experience this side of the night. I was lonely, sure, but that could always change. Loneliness is not permanent.

The cobblestone path ended in a short alley. The alley was kept immaculately clean, for it provided convenient access to the many shops and restaurants. At the moment, the alley was empty and dark. The lights were out. Or broken. I was willing to bet broken. I had long ago lost my fear of dark alleys. My footfalls reverberated off the high walls of the surrounding businesses. I passed behind the back entrance to a used bookstore, a comic book shop, a stationary store and a pet store. The Downtown Grill was the only establishment open at this hour. Music pumped from the restaurant's open door. Fire escapes crowded the air space above the alley like oversized cobwebs.

# Moon Dance

Sitting on the fire escape was a woman. Pointing a gun at me.

There was a flash, followed immediately by a muffled shot. Something exploded in my chest and I staggered backward. I kept my balance and looked down. Dark blood trickled from a hole in my dress. Next came two more muffled shots—and the impact of two more bullets turned me almost completely around. The bullets had been neatly placed in my stomach. Some good shooting. My red dress was ruined.

The woman walked casually down the fire escape. I saw that there was a silencer on the gun. No one would have heard the muffled shots, especially above the din of music pumping from the restaurant. The fire escape creaked under her weight.

From out of the shadows emerged Sara Benson, Kingsley's receptionist. She paused in the alley and held the gun in both hands like a pro. Her hair was pulled back tightly, revealing every inch of her beautiful face. Her eyes were wide and lustful, and tonight she appeared particularly radiant. Her shapely legs were spaced evenly at shoulder width. A good shooting stance. Any attorney should be so lucky to have such a beautiful receptionist.

Except this receptionist had gone over the edge.

"How could you help that animal, Mrs. Moon?" she said. Her voice was even, and calculating, as if her words had been planned well in advance. I could hear again the undercurrent of rage and hatred, and now I understood fully who that anger was directed toward.

I assumed she was talking about Kingsley. "He's not an animal," I said. Actually, technically, she might have had a point there.

She paused, no doubt surprised that I was still speaking. Her surprise quickly turned into indignant, self-righteous rant. "Not an animal? Murderers have been set free, rapists have been let loose. The man has no conscious. He's manipulative and horrible."

"He's just doing his job."

"He does it too well."

"Perhaps. But that's neither for you nor I to decide. There's safeguards put into place in the law to protect the innocent. He upholds these safeguards. Not everyone in prison belongs in prison."

She shook her head, and continued moving closer. I could see tears streaming down her face. Why the hell was *she* getting so emotional? Wasn't *I* the one getting shot here?

"I love him," she said. "There is something so different about him, and I wanted to be part of that. I would have done anything for him. I gave him everything in my heart, but still he left me. And now he has you."

"Let me guess. If you can't have him, then no one can?"

She cocked her head and fired her weapon again. My head snapped back. Blood poured down the bridge of my nose. I'll give her this much: she was a hell of a shot. Which didn't surprise me much, since she was also a hell of an athlete.

*And able to leap small park benches in a single bound.*

For a brief second, my vision doubled and then even trebled, then everything righted itself once again. Three seconds later the bullet in my head emerged and dropped into my open palm.

Let's see Copperfield do *that*.

Sara stared at me in dumbfounded shock.

221

From the opposite end of the alley, coming up from the Commonwealth Avenue entrance, another figure appeared. A very large and burly figure. He was standing in a small pool of light from the alley opening.

"Stop!" shouted Detective Sherbet. "Drop your weapon. Now!"

But Sara didn't drop her weapon. Instead, she swung her arm around with the gun.

I jumped forward. "Sara, don't!"

Too late. She didn't get all the way around. Three gunshots exploded from Sherbet's end of the alley. His shots weren't muffled by a silencer. The echoes cracked and thundered down the narrow corridor, assaulting the eardrums.

Sara pirouetted like a ballerina, spinning on one heel. Her gun flung off in one direction and her shoe in the other. And as the sound of Sherbet's pistol still reverberated in the alley, Sara's last dance was over and she collapsed.

Sherbet dashed over to us. He was out of breath and looking quite pale. As he reached down for Sara he called for backup and an ambulance.

Then he looked up at me for the first time. "You okay, Sam—" And then he stopped short. "Sweet Jesus. You've been shot."

"Really? I hadn't noticed."

"The ambulance is on its way."

"Won't be necessary."

He was silent for a long time. In the distance, I heard the coming sirens.

"We will definitely be talking, Samantha."

"I expect so, Detective."

# 63.

Rain drizzled outside Kingsley's open French windows.

Water gurgled forth from the fountain with the breasts. Kingsley and I were sitting together on his leather couch. Our shoulders touched. There seemed to be a sort of kinetic energy between us. A sexual energy. At least, there was a sexual energy in *me*.

"Tell me how you figured out Sara was the shooter," he said.

"Three things. First, Horton was in constant contact with her, especially in the hours prior to each shooting. Second, she contacted me from her cell number, claiming she was calling from work, which I found odd. Third, I recalled the picture on her desk, the one taken at the office Halloween party. She went as a pirate."

Kingsley smacked his forehead with his palm. "The mustache. Good Lord, I've seen that picture a hundred times."

"It's the spitting image of your shooter."

"But why didn't you suspect her earlier? I thought you had some sort of ESP thing going on?"

"I do. But it's not an exact science. I sensed a lot of anger from Sara, but I assumed that anger was directed at her failed relationship with you."

"Granted most of my relationships have been failures since the death of my wife, but how did you know about Sara and me?"

"I'm an ace detective, remember?"

"Yes, but—"

"She hinted at it."

"Okay, yeah, we dated. We hit it off initially, but things didn't quite take."

"Ya think?"

We drank some more wine. Our shoulders continued touching.

"Speaking of dating," I said. "Danny's secretary dumped him."

"Is that why you can't wipe that smile off your face?"

"It's one of the reasons," I said. "Not to mention Horton has admitted Sara approached him with a proposal to kill you and your client. He provided the gun and surveillance. She did the shooting."

"Then why attack me in broad daylight, in front of so many witnesses?"

"That was calculated. The shooting was scheduled between security shifts; her getaway truck was parked nearby, the plates removed. Horton was waiting a few blocks away, where they swapped cars. The truck was then concealed in a parking garage." I paused and sipped from my Chardonnay. Even vampires get dry mouths. "Now, with Sara dead and the game up, Horton confessed to everything. He will stand trial as an accessory to murder and attempted murder."

We were silent. Kingsley reached over and gently took my hand. His hand was comforting. And damn big. The rain picked up a little and *plinked* against the French windows.

"You did good work," said Kingsley. "You were worth every penny."

"Of which you still owe me a few."

"When I get my new secretary I'll have her write you a check." He took my wine glass and walked over to his bar and filled me up. From the bar, he said, "I did some research on the medallion."

I perked up. "And?"

"The medallion is rumored to be connected to a way of reversing the effects of vampirism."

"Reversing?" I said, "I don't understand."

"The medallion," he said, "coupled with some very powerful magicks, can *reverse* vampirism."

"You mean—"

"You would be mortal again, Sam. That is, if we're talking about the same medallion, which, by the way, is highly coveted, so you might want to keep this on the down low."

My head was swimming with the possibilities. To be human again. To be *normal* again. To have my kids again.

I looked over at Kingsley and there was real pain on his face. He was hurting.

"What's wrong?" I asked.

"Isn't it obvious?" he asked.

"You think that if I choose to be mortal..." my voice trailed off.

"I would lose you," he said, finishing. "And I wouldn't blame you for one second."

I stood and came to him, this beautiful, massive man who made me feel alive again, who made me feel sexy again, who made me feel human again, even when I was at my lowest. I sat down in his huge, warm lap and put my arms around his huge, warm neck. I leaned in and pressed my lips softly against his.

When I pulled away after a long moment, I said, "And what if I told you I was falling in love with you?"

"Then that would make me the happiest man, or half-man, on earth," he said. "But what about being mortal again?"

"We'll look into that another day."

"Good idea."

And he kissed me deeply, powerfully, his lips and tongue taking me in completely.

It was a hell of a kiss.

# 64.

*Did I catch you at a good time, Fang?*

*It's always a good time when I hear from you, Moon Dance.*

*No girls over tonight?*

*No girls for awhile. So what's new in your world, Moon Dance?*

So I told him. I wrote it up quickly in one long, mangled paragraph.

*More type-o's than a blood bank,* he answered when I had finished. *I think Sara truly loved Kingsley, at least in her own twisted way.*

*Loved him and hated him.*

*And it drove her to a certain madness.*

*Yes,* I wrote, remembering Sara's pirouetting body. Watching her land in a heap as a pool of dark blood spread around her. I had stared deep into that dark pool, and felt a hunger.

Fang wrote: *She thought Kingsley morally reprehensible, which justified her attempt on his life. And she would have succeeded had he not been immortal. You immortals get all the breaks.*

*Some of them,* I wrote.

*Rejection can make you do some crazy things.*

# Moon Dance

*Like jump off a hotel balcony,* I added.

*Yes. But not everyone has wings.*

*So why no girls for awhile, Fang?*

*Because I was in love with another woman.*

*So who's the lucky woman?*

There was a long delay. A very long delay. I wrote: *Fang?*

And then on my computer screen appeared a single red rose, followed by the words: *I love you, Moon Dance.*

I stared at my monitor. More words appeared.

*I fell in love with you instantly. I know this sounds crazy because I've never met you, but I have fallen in love with the image I have created of you in my mind. There will never be a woman on the face of this earth who can compare to this image. All will fall short.*

He stopped writing, and I read his words over and over again. Finally, I wrote my response.

*We are both crazy, Fang. You know that, right?*

*Yes, I know that.*

*Goodnight, Fang.*

*Goodnight, Moon Dance.*

Coming Soon

I SING THE BODY DEPARTED
A Ghost Story

by

J.R. Rain

# Moon Dance

# 1.

I stepped through the wall and into my daughter's bedroom.

She was sleeping contentedly on her side. It was before dawn and the building was quiet. The curtains were open and the sky was black beyond. If there were any stars, they were lost to the L.A. smog. The curtains were covered with ponies, as was most of the room. A plastic pony light switch, a pony bed lamp, pony wallpaper and bedspread. Someday she would outgrow her obsession with ponies, although I secretly hoped not.

*A girl and her pony. It's a beautiful thing.*

I stepped closer to my sleeping daughter, and as I did so she shifted slightly towards me. She mewed like a newborn kitten. Crimson light from her alarm clock splashed over her delicate features, highlighting a slightly upturned nose and impossibly big eyes. Sometimes when she slept her closed eyelids fluttered and danced. But not tonight. Tonight she was sleeping deeply, no doubt dreaming of sugar and spice and everything nice.

Or of Barbies and boys and everything in-between.

I wondered if she ever dreamed of me. I'm sure she did at times. Were those dreams good or bad? Did she ever wake up sad and missing her father?

*Do you* want *her to wake up sad?* I asked myself.

*No*, I thought. *I wanted her to wake up rested, restored and full of peace.*

I stepped away from the far wall and glided over to the small chair in the corner of her room. We had made the chair together one weekend, a father/daughter project for the Girl's Scouts. To her credit, she did most of the work.

I sat in it now, lowering my weightless body into it, mimicking the act of sitting. Unsurprisingly, the chair didn't creak.

As I sat, my daughter rolled over in her sleep, facing me. Her aura, usually blue and streaked with red flames, often reacted to my presence, as it did now. The red flames crackled and gravitated toward me like a pulsating static ball, sensing me like I sensed it.

As I continued to sit, the lapping red flames grew in intensity, snapping and licking the air like solar flares on the surface of the sun. My daughter's aura always reacted this way to me. But only in sleep. Somehow her subconscious recognized, or perhaps it was her soul. Or both. And from this subconscious state, she would sometimes speak to me, as she did now.

"Hi, daddy."

"Hi, baby," I said.

"Mommy said you got hurt real bad."

"Yes, I did."

"Mommy said that a bad man hurt you and you got killed."

"Mommy's right, but I don't want you thinking about that right now, okay?"

"Okay," she said sleepily. "Am I dreaming, daddy?"

"Yes, baby."

We were quiet and she shifted subtly, lifting her face toward me, her eyes still closed in sleep. There was a sound from outside her window, a light tapping. I ignored it, but it came again and again, and then with more consistency. I looked over my shoulder and saw that it was raining. I looked back at my daughter and thought of the rain, remembering how it felt on my skin, on my face. Or, rather, I was *trying* to remember. Lately, such memories of the flesh were getting harder and harder to recall.

"It's raining, daddy," she said.

"Yes."

"Do you live in the rain?"

"No."

"Where do you live, daddy?"

"I live here, with you."

"But you're dead."

I said nothing. I hated to be reminded of this, even by my daughter.

"Why don't you go to heaven, daddy?"

I thought about that. I think about that a lot, actually. I said, "Daddy still has work to do."

"What kind of work?"

"Good work."

"I miss you," she said. "I miss you so much. I think about you every day. I'm always crying. People at school say I'm a crybaby."

"You're not a crybaby," I said. "You're just sad." My heart broke all over again. "It's time to go back to sleep, angel."

"Okay, daddy."

"I love you, sweetie."

"I love you, too, daddy."

I drifted up from the small wooden chair and moved across the room the way I do—silently and easily—and at the far wall I looked back at her. Her aura had subsided, although some of it still flared here and there. For her to relax—to truly relax—I needed to leave her room entirely.

And so I did. Through the wall.

To hell with doors.

# 2.

I was standing behind him, reading the newspaper from over his shoulder, as I did every morning.

His name was Jerrold and he was close to sixty and close to retirement. He lived alone and seemed mostly happy. He was addicted to internet poker, but, as far as I could tell, that was his only vice.

*Thank God.*

He turned the paper casually, snapping it taught, then reached for his steaming mug of coffee, heavy with sugar and cream, and took a long sip. I could smell the coffee. Or at least a *hint* of it, just like I could smell a hint of his aftershave and hair gel. My senses were weak at best.

As he set the mug down, some of the coffee sloshed over the rim and onto the back of his hand. He yelped and shook his hand. I could see that it had immediately reddened.

*Pain.*

I hadn't known pain in quite a long time. My last memory of it was when I had been working at a friend's house, cutting carpet, and nearly severed my arm off.

I looked down at my translucent arm now. Although nearly imperceptible, the scar was still there—or at least the ghostly hint of it.

Still cursing under his breath, Jerrold turned back to his paper. So did I. He scanned the major headlines, and I scanned them along with him. After all, he was my hands in this situation.

He read through some local Los Angeles news, mostly political stuff that would have bored me to tears had I tears to be bored with. I glanced over at his coffee while he read, trying to remember what it tasted like. I think I remembered.

*I think.*

Hot, roasted, bitter and sweet. I knew the words, but I was having a hard time recalling the actual flavor. That scared me.

Jerrold turned the page. As he did so, something immediately caught my eye; luckily, it caught his eye, too.

A piano teacher had been murdered at St. Luke's, a converted monastery that was now being used as a Catholic church and school. Lucy Randolph was eighty-six years old and just three days shy from celebrating her sixtieth anniversary with her husband.

I had known Mrs. Randolph. In fact, she had been my own music teacher back when I was a student at St. Luke's. She had been kind to a fault, a source of inspiration and joy to her students, and especially to me.

And now, according to the report, someone had strangled her, leaving her for dead on the very piano she had taught from. Perhaps the very same piano *I* had been taught from.

*Damn.*

Jerrold clucked his tongue and shook his head and moved on to the next page, but I had seen enough. I stepped away,

"You're still young, Jerrold," I said to him. "Lose fifteen pounds and find someone special--and ditch the gambling."

# Moon Dance

As I spoke, the small hairs on the back of his neck stood up and and his aura shifted towards me. He shivered unconsciously and turned the page.

I left his apartment.

# 3.

We were in Pauline's apartment.

She was drinking an apple martini and I wasn't, which was a damn shame. At the moment, I was sitting in an old wingback chair and she was on the couch, one bare foot up on a hand-painted coffee table which could have doubled for a modern piece of abstract art.

"If you ever need any extra money," I said, "you could always sell your coffee table on eBay."

"It's not for sale," she said. "Ever."

"What if you were homeless and living on the streets and needed money?"

"Then I would be homeless and living on the streets with the world's most bitchen hand-painted coffee table."

Her name was Pauline and she was a world-famous medium. She could hear me, see me and sometimes even touch me. Hell, she could even read my thoughts, which was a bit disconcerting for me. She was a full-figured woman, with perhaps the most beautiful face I had ever seen. She often wore her long brown hair haphazardly, a look that would surely have your average California girl running back to the bathroom mirror. Pauline was not your average California girl. She wasn't your average girl by any definition, spending as much of her time in the world of the dead as in the world of the living. Luckily, she just so happened to live in the very building I was presently haunting.

"Yeah, lucky me," said Pauline, picking up on my thoughts.

She did her readings out of a small office near downtown Los Angeles, usually working with just one or two clients a day. Some of her sessions lasted longer than others and tonight she was home later than usual, hitting the booze hard, as she often did. I wouldn't call her a drunk, but she was damn close to being one.

"I'm not a drunk," Pauline said absently, reading my thoughts again. "I can stop any time I want. The booze just helps me...release."

"Release?" I asked.

"Yeah, to forget. To unwind. To *un*everything."

"You should probably not drink so much," I said.

She regarded me over her martini glass. Her eyes were bloodshot. Her face gleamed with a fine film of sweat. She wasn't as attractive when she was drunk.

"Thanks," she said sarcastically. "And do you even remember what it's like being drunk?"

I thought about that. "A little. And that was below the belt."

"Do you even have a belt?"

I looked down at my slightly glowing ethereal body. Hell, even my clothing glowed, which was the same clothing I had been wearing on the night I was murdered two years ago: a white tee shirt and long red basketball shorts, my usual sleeping garb. I was barefoot and I suspected my hair was a mess, since I had been shot to death in my sleep. Dotting my body were the various bloody holes where the bullets had long ago entered my living flesh.

"No belt," I said. "Then again, no shoes, either."

She laughed, which caused some of her martini to slosh over the rim. She cursed and licked her fingers like a true alcoholic.

"Oh, shut up," she said.

"Waste not, want not," I said.

She glared at me some more as she took a long pull on her drink. When she set it down, she missed the center of the cork coaster by about three inches. Now part of the glass sat askew on the edge of the coaster, and the whole thing looked like it might tip over. She didn't notice or care.

Pauline worked with spirits all day. Early on, she had tried her best to ignore my presence. But I knew she could see me, and so I pursued her relentlessly until she finally acknowledged my existence.

"And now I can't get rid of you," she said.

"You love me," I said. "Admit it."

"Yeah," she said. "I do. Call me an idiot, but I do."

"Idiot," I said. "Besides, I'm different than those other ghosts."

"Yeah? How so?"

"I'm a ghost on a mission."

"Could that sound more corny?" she said.

"Maybe after a few more drinks," I said.

"So how's the mission coming along?" she asked. We had been over this before, perhaps dozens of times.

"I don't know," I said. "It's not like I'm getting a lot of feedback from anyone—or anything."

"And when will you be done with your mission?" she asked.

"I don't know that either."

"And what, exactly, is your mission?" As she spoke, she peered into the empty glass with one eye.

"To save my soul."

"Oh, yeah, that. And you're sure it's not too late to save your soul? I mean, you are dead after all."

"It's never too late," I said.

"And you know that how?" she asked.

"Because I'm not in hell yet."

"You're haunting an old apartment building in Los Angeles," she said. "Sounds a bit like hell to me."

"But I can see my wife and daughter whenever I want," I countered. "Can't be that bad."

"Your wife has re-married," said Pauline. "And weren't you two separated at the time of your death?"

We had been, but the details of our separation were lost to me. We had financial problems I seemed to recall, which had led to many arguments. What we had argued about was anyone's guess. But the arguments had been heated and impassioned and in the end I had moved out—but not very far. To stay close to my daughter, I had rented an apartment in the same building.

"Yes, we had been separated," I said. "And thank you for reminding me of that."

"Just keeping it real," said Pauline indifferently. "Besides, there is no hell."

"How do you know?"

"I talk to the dead, remember? And not just ghosts," she added. "But those who have passed on."

"Passed on to heaven?" I asked.

"Passed on to *something*," she said. "Neither heaven nor hell. A spirit world—and it's waiting for you."

I didn't believe that. I believed in heaven and hell, and I was certain, as of this moment, that I was going to hell. "Well, it can keep on waiting. I'm not ready to pass on."

"Obviously."

"I need to work some things out," I said.

"And then what?" she asked.

"And then I will accept my fate."

She nodded. "But for now you hope to change your fate."

"Yes."

She looked at me with bloodshot eyes. Sitting on the couch, she had tucked her bare feet under her. Now her painted red toes peaked out like frightened little mice.

"Nice imagery," she said, wiggling her toes. "So you still can't remember why you are going to hell?"

"No," I said.

"But it was something bad."

"Very bad," I said.

"Bad enough to burn forever?" she asked.

"Somebody died, I think."

"So you've said, but you still don't remember who or why."

I shook my head. "No, but it happened a long, long time ago."

"And with your death," she added, "it was the first of your memories to disappear."

She was right. My memories were disappearing at an alarming rate. The earlier memories of my life were mostly long gone. "Yeah, something like that," I said.

"And now you're afraid to pass on because you think you are going to hell, even though you can't remember *why* you are going to hell."

"It's a hell of a conundrum," I said.

She nodded, then got up, padded into the adjoining kitchen, and poured herself another drink. When she came back and sat, some of her drink splashed over the rim of her glass.

"Don't say a word," she cautioned me.

I laughed and drifted over to the big bay window and looked out over Los Angeles, which glittered and pulsed five stories below. At this hour, Los Feliz Boulevard was a parking lot dotted with red brake lights as far as the eye could see. I had heard once that it was one of the busiest streets in the world. Standing here now, I believed it.

After a while, Pauline came over and stood next to me. Actually, some of her was standing *inside* me. She shivered with the sensation, apologized, and stepped back. Ghostly etiquette.

I thought of my sweet music teacher. According to the paper, she had been just days away from her sixtieth wedding anniversary. *Sixtieth.*

Anger welled up within me. As it did so, a rare warmth spread through me. Mostly my days were filled with bone-chilling cold, minus the bones. But whenever strong emotion was involved, such as anger, I became flush with energy. And when that happened—

"Hey," said Pauline. "Someone's making a rare appearance."

And so I was. So much so that I could actually see myself reflecting in the big, sliding glass door. Next to me was Pauline, looking beautiful, but drunk. Bloody wounds covered my body; in particular, my forehead, neck and chest.

I didn't get to see myself often, and, despite my anger, I took advantage of this rare opportunity. Pale and ethereal, I was just a vague suggestion of what I had once been—and I was growing vaguer as the years pressed on. There was stubble on my jaw, and my dark hair was indeed askew. Eternal bed head.

*Great.*

"But you're still a cutie," said Pauline, giggling, now almost entirely drunk.

And with those words and that infectious giggle, my anger abated and I started fading away again.

"Tell me about your murdered friend," said Pauline.

"She wasn't necessarily a friend."

She explored my mind a bit more. "My apologies. Your piano teacher from grade school."

"Yes."

"Why would someone kill her?" she asked.

"I don't know."

She paused, then nodded knowingly. "I see you intend to find out."

"Yes."

"And perhaps save your soul in the process?"

"That's the plan," I said. "For now."

"You do realize you have limits to where you can go and what you can do, right?"

I shrugged. "Minor technicalities."

## About the Author:

J.R. Rain lives in a small house on a small island with his small dog, Sadie, who has more energy than Robin Williams.

# Moon Dance

Made in the USA
Lexington, KY
22 February 2010